THE HOLIDAY PRIZE

THE HAWAIIAN GETAWAY SERIES
BOOK 4

MEGAN REINKING

CONTENTS

For anyone who finds themselves feeling lonely or in need of a friend this holiday season. I hope this book brings you some joy and a smile to your face.

1

TORI

The snowball leaves a sharp sting the moment it touches my cheek, sending a trail of cold, wet snow sliding down the right side of my face.

"Ah! You got me," I laugh, scooping up a handful of snow with my gloved hands to toss back at my assailant—my eight-year-old nephew, Elliot. "Nice shot, buddy. But it's going to take a lot more than that to take this zombie down."

"Bring it on. I'm the best zombie fighter this world has ever seen," he growls in the most threatening voice he can muster. I push my lips together to hide a smile. I can tell he's been practicing. This is the closest he's come to imitating the main character of that zombie-apocalypse movie he's been obsessing over all week. He wipes at his face with the arm of his down jacket, causing his already haphazard hat to push even farther up on his head, fully exposing one of his ears to the harsh Minnesota wind.

"Elliot, ears!" my brother, Matt, calls from the barely cracked front window of his in-laws' house. We've somehow scrambled our way toward the very farthest corner of the front yard, so I add in a quick reminder of my own in case he didn't hear.

"Ugh," Elliot huffs in response to the interruption, complete with a slight eye roll, as he roughly pulls the hat back down before picking up another clump of snow. He launches it at the center of my back as I squeal. My borrowed boots feel extra heavy and one size too big as I attempt to run through the six inches of freshly fallen snow. I stumble, exhaustion catching up to me, and I suddenly feel like I've run straight into a brick wall.

"Okay, fine. Truce! I surrender." I collapse onto the snow, spreading my limbs out like a starfish. Elliot hurries over to stand in front of me, doing his best to look menacing.

"Say it," he demands, aiming his pretend sword directly at my throat. His eyebrows are furrowed, and his nose is scrunched in an impressive display of faux anger.

"Say what?" I ask, my breath still labored, knowing full well what he wants me to say.

"You know. Say it," he demands again.

"Fine." I raise my hands in a slow show of defeat. "You're the greatest zombie slayer in all of the land. I never stood a chance. You are far superior."

"Yes," he hisses in victory, pumping his fists in the air before dropping to lie next to me with a laugh. His feeble attempt to quiet his giggles makes me start to giggle too. After a few moments of lazily snickering at each other, I turn my head to look at him with a lingering smile on my face.

"So, Elliot," I say, my voice back to normal. "We've been here for a week now. What would you say is the best thing we've done so far on our break?"

Matt's wife, Paige's, family lives in Minnesota, and despite the colder weather, I decided to tag along with them on their trip here over Thanksgiving break. It's been a fun week indulging in early winter activities and snow that we don't have back at home on Oahu.

"Hm. Probably snow tubing at the big ski hill. Or no! Maybe the snowman family that Dad and I created over there." He points to the opposite corner of the yard where there are two large 'adult' snowmen, each flanked by a smaller 'child' snowman. "I think they turned out pretty great—even if they are a little lopsided."

"Any luck convincing your mom and dad to get you a puppy?" I ask, eyeing the rectangular lump of snow that Elliot says is the dog they don't have yet.

"No." He frowns. "They keep saying maybe next year. Once Noelle is a little bit older."

"That makes sense," I say, giving him a sympathetic smile. "It's hard to wait when you really want something, though, isn't it?"

"Yeah," he agrees with a sad nod.

Elliot came into our life just a couple years ago when Matt married Paige. Paige was Elliot's foster parent for a while, and after they got married, she and Matt officially adopted him. The three of them and their two-year-old daughter, Noelle, are the ones I'm closest to in my family. Not that I'm not close with everybody, because I am. In addition to Matt and Paige, I have three sisters, my parents, a slew of brothers-in-law, and another niece. Our entire family is loud, boisterous, and filled with oversharing, boundary-crossing, meddling people—and I love every single one of them.

As close as I am to all of them, I do spend most of my time with Matt's family—especially Elliot. I'm proud of the relationship we've created. He's one of the most caring, thoughtful, and straightforward kids I've ever met, and his bluntness makes him one of my favorite people in the world to talk to.

"Hey, you guys want to come inside and warm up?" Matt asks, stepping onto the front porch. "It's almost time to eat."

"Sure, Dad!" Elliot hops up and then grabs my arms to help pull me up.

"Thanks, buddy," I mumble, finding my footing in the snow.

I trail behind Elliot as we trudge through the thickness, eventually finding and following the sidewalk that leads up to the front porch. We climb the steps and stomp our feet on the mat before slipping past Matt into the house.

"Wait until you try the mashed potatoes," Matt says, leaning back to fish out a beer from the case that's wedged in the snowbank—or makeshift cooler—before following us inside. "I almost lost my finger when I snuck a taste."

"That's because you probably didn't wash your hands first, and Mom didn't want you spreading germs," Elliot points out matter-of-factly.

"He has a point," I laugh, unclasping the shoulder strap of my snow pants while Matt playfully rolls his eyes, crouching to help Elliot take off his boots.

We shed our layers of winter gear, toss them into the dryer, and then I quickly run my fingers through my hair before following them through the living room to the dining area.

"Oh, perfect timing! Dinner is ready. Let's eat before it gets cold," Paige's mom, Denise, says, wedging the dish of glazed carrots between the turkey and the stuffing, finishing off the Thanksgiving tablescape like a beautiful last piece of a puzzle. Small, artificial, white pumpkins and brown and orange foliage are tucked in between each dish, covering the span of the table. She slides into a seat at the table where Paige's dad and brother are already sitting. I take a seat between Paige and Elliot as Matt settles Noelle into a booster seat.

"Everything looks delicious," I say, admiring the feast. "Sorry I wasn't much help in the kitchen. I meant to come in earlier, but time got away from me."

"Oh, no worries." Paige smiles with a wave of her hand. "Thanks for keeping Elliot entertained. I've gotten my butt kicked in Zombieland out there enough times this week. I needed a break."

"Hey, I let you win once," Elliot points out.

"And that was very kind of you." Paige winks at him.

Denise starts passing the serving dishes one by one. First, the basket of rolls, followed by the cranberries, turkey, mashed potatoes, stuffing, carrots, and my personal favorite—sweet potato casserole, complete with marshmallows melted over the top.

"Well, I have to say again, I am just so grateful that you all came to Minnesota for Thanksgiving. The weather is hit-or-miss here this time of year, and obviously, Hawaii is a tropical paradise year-round. We truly do appreciate you traveling all this way." Denise holds a hand to her chest as she gives a grateful smile.

"Can we come back over Christmas break too?" Elliot asks Matt with hopeful eyes.

"I don't think your other grandma would appreciate us missing two holidays in a row with them," Matt laughs, ruffling the top of his head.

"You're right about that," I add in agreement. "Sorry, Elliot."

"Have you been enjoying your time off from work, Tori?" Denise asks once our food has all been plated. "From what Paige tells me, you're a very successful real estate agent."

"She's the best agent on the whole island," Paige says before I have a chance to reply.

"I don't know if I would say that..." I start, my cheeks flushing with the attention.

"It's true," Elliot chimes in. "Nana Janice says Auntie Tori is married to her work, and that's why she's not married to an actual person yet."

To anyone else, that comment might cause them to roll their eyes, but given that it's a sentiment I've heard continuously since the day I turned twenty-five, I barely bat an eye. At twenty-six now, I've had a whole year to become essentially numb to the unsolicited comments garnered from my mom and sisters.

"Nothing wrong with that," Matt says, shoveling a forkful of turkey in his mouth. As a typical older brother, he's always been overly critical of anyone my sisters and I have dated, so he's pretty much the only family member that's just as fine as I am with me being single.

"Yes, I am enjoying the time away. Although, I've still been able to get a few things done from my computer this past week. The market has been on fire this year, so it's been non-stop. I haven't had a chance to take a true break." I scoop up some cranberry sauce, mix it with a bite of turkey, and savor the contrast of savory and tart flavors.

"Oh, that's wonderful, Tori," she replies, and we share a sincere smile before moving on.

"Elliot, do you still want to try out that snowshoe trail tomorrow?" I ask. "We only have a couple days left before we fly home, so it's now or never."

"Absolutely!" he says with so much enthusiasm that we all laugh. His excitement and up-for-anything attitude have been refreshing and contagious this whole trip.

When we're sufficiently stuffed full, I help bus dishes to the kitchen and pitch in with cleaning up. I scoop leftovers into containers and help load the dishwasher alongside Denise, making small-talk chatter as we work. After the clean-up is mostly done, we gather back around the kitchen table.

"Alright," Paige says, a paring knife in hand. "I have a very important question. Pumpkin or banana cream pie?"

Later that evening, after a hot shower, I rub some vanilla bean-scented lotion onto my hands and slide into the warm flannel sheets that are on Paige's childhood bed. I pick at a loose strand at the corner of an embroidered flower on the duvet cover, flatten the top of it with my hands, and grab my laptop off the nightstand to bring to my lap. After it powers on, I log into my work software, where I immediately find four pop-up messages from my friend and fellow agent, Connor.

Connor: Tell me you checked your email.

Connor: Have you checked your email yet?

Connor: Happy Thanksgiving, by the way.

Connor: Read it and call me ASAP.

"What the…" I mumble in confusion as I open my inbox and find several unopened emails. The one from Brad, the founder and CEO of the brokerage firm I work for that has 'Happy Thanksgiving and Urgent Request' in the subject line catches my eye. Intrigued, I open it.

From: Brad@covestocondosrealty.com
To: You, and 45 others

Greetings everyone,
My apologies for sending work correspondence on a holiday, but something has transpired this afternoon, and given its time-sensitive nature, I felt it was necessary to reach out as soon as possible.
As you all know, my listing of Makana Manor has been sitting

idle for the majority of this year (due in large part to Mr.
Sherwood's refusal to take my advice and come down from his
high twenty-three million dollar listing price).

After a conversation with Mr. Sherwood this morning, it is
apparent that he has become irritated with the lack of interest. He
is threatening to walk and list with another firm if it is not sold
for the full asking price by the end of the year. I have grown
frustrated with this listing, and my hands are full with my current
workload as well as other end-of-the-year tasks, so I'm
hypothetically removing myself as the lead selling agent on this
listing. This email is to officially issue a challenge to any agent
who is interested in taking a crack at it.

I will still be the listing agent on paper, but the agent or agent(s)
who bring me a full-ask buyer before January 1st will not only
receive the commission but also a bonus that I am personally
offering of fifty-thousand dollars.

You have my permission to use any tactics (legally, of course)
and do whatever it takes to sell this house. Mr. Sherwood is a
very important client, and it is in the best interest of the entire
firm to do anything it takes to keep him as one. Let me know if
you have any further questions.

Happy Thanksgiving,
Brad

No. No, no, no, no.

Several different profanities come to mind as I finish reading
the email and realize that the biggest listing in our agency—the
one that every single one of us has drooled over for the past year
—is now up for grabs, and I'm currently about four thousand
miles away. Away from my desk and all the resources I have at
the office.

I immediately close out the email and pull up the website for the airline company. I'll have to make it up to Elliot once we're back home, because there's no way I'll be going snowshoeing tomorrow—I'll be on the earliest flight back to Oahu.

2

TORI

Clutching the large pile of mail close to my chest, I swing my mailbox door shut and twist the key to lock and close it. Grabbing my suitcase, I roll my way to the elevator on the far side of the spacious lobby of my oceanfront condo building.

"Six?" a woman guesses as I squeeze in next to her. I don't know her well, but I do recognize her as someone who also lives in the building. Despite the fact that we've crossed paths many times, and I pride myself on being personable, there are somehow only two things that I know about this woman. She's almost always sipping a coffee from Julie's Coffee Shop when I see her, and she lives on the ninth floor.

"Yes, please," I say politely with a nod.

The elevator doors shut, she looks down at her phone, and we spend the ride up in comfortable silence. I've lived in this building for about three years now, and while I've met quite a few of my neighbors, and everyone has been very friendly, we all mostly keep to ourselves. Surface-level niceties and gestures are the extent of my relationship with anyone who lives in this building, and we live in a quiet, pleasant environment—just the way I like it. I do get the urge to get to know my neighbors more every once in a while, but we've gotten so used to this dynamic of living our lives parallel to each other that no one seems to ever take it a step further. It's almost like nobody wants to start a ripple effect that could come with a deeper relationship and risk disrupting the good, symbiotic environment we've created.

"Have a great day." I smile before it comes to a complete stop on the sixth floor, feeling anxious to keep moving.

"You too." She looks up briefly to smile as I roll my suitcase out and down the hallway. When I reach unit 624, I shuffle things around in my arms just enough to unlock and push the door open with one hand. Leaving my luggage leaning up against the wall behind the door, I slide my slip-on tennis shoes off. My bare feet feel cold against the light-gray tile floor that extends from my entryway and covers the entire length of my unit.

I drop my keys and mail on the black countertops that sit above the off-white cabinets in my kitchen, then rush past the living area and down the hall to my bedroom. Determined to get to the office as soon as I possibly can, I hastily change out of my travel clothes, pulling on a pair of dark-wash jean capris, tuck in a loose white T-shirt, and throw a lightweight cream blazer over the top to finish off the outfit before digging a pair of strappy sandals out of my closet.

Perched on the corner of my heavily blanketed bed, I slip them on. A throw pillow falls out of place, so I carefully put it back on top of the perfectly placed mountain of cushions that live on my bed when I'm not inside of it.

My home is my refuge. When I bought my condo three years ago, my top mission was to make it feel like a sanctuary. A comfy, soul-fueling place to recharge at the end of the day. Every single decor choice was made with intention. From the lush green plants that are scattered around to the numerous picture frames filled with memories and people I love, everything serves me in some way.

After a brief stop in the bathroom, where I attempt to tame my wavy blonde curls by running a brush through them, I eventually decide it's as good as it's going to get after traveling overnight on the red-eye. Before I grab my keys, I sift quickly through the pile of mail next to them to see if there's anything important. I filter through an assortment of bills and junk mail until a 5 x 8 white envelope drops out onto the counter. My name and address are printed in beautiful calligraphy on the front. Immediately assuming it's a Christmas card, I rip it open, wondering who has their act together enough to already be sending them out so early in the season.

The thought alone warms my heart. Receiving cards in the mail is one of my very favorite aspects of the holiday season. The first one is always the most special, for no other reason other than it signifies all the others to come—the beginning of something beautiful that's about to unfold.

Confusion takes over when I pull the card out and find a man and a woman in the middle of what looks to be a hiking trail, the burnt-orange, red, and green colors of the fall leaves on display surrounding them. *Wishing you the merriest holiday season! Love, The Clarks.* It's a beautiful picture, and I appreciate the sentiment, but I'm stuck on one thing—I've never met these people in my life.

I pick up the envelope to make sure it wasn't delivered to the wrong person, but nope, my name and address are indeed written on the front. When I eye the return address, I see that The Clarks live in Fayetteville, Arkansas. They don't look familiar to me whatsoever, but maybe they're previous clients of mine that moved away from Hawaii, and I somehow don't remember. Or maybe they're relatives of one of my siblings' spouses. I find it odd, but I shake my head, not having the time to focus on it right now. Leaving the card on the counter, I grab my keys and purse.

The entire walk out of my unit and down the elevator is spent staring at my phone, scrolling, and catching up on work emails. When I push the front doors of the condo building open, I'm immediately hit with a wave of humid, hot air. A ray of sunshine obstructs my vision, so I slide my sunglasses on, taking a left onto the sidewalk. The brokerage firm is only two blocks from my condo, so on the days when I need to be in the office, I typically walk there to soak up as much sunshine as I possibly can.

Large groups of bikini-clad people with beach bags and coolers walk past me, heading in the opposite direction toward the beach. Heat from the sun burns onto the back of my neck as I walk, my hair just starting to stick to my skin. When I pull open the entrance doors of my work, I'm relieved to be greeted with a pleasant rush of cool air.

"Morning, Tori." Our friendly receptionist, Ellen, smiles in greeting as she looks up from her computer. Her reading glasses are pushed up onto the top of her head, holding some of her short, sandy-blonde hair back in place.

"Hi, Ellen. How was your Thanksgiving?" I pause at her semi-circle desk that faces the front doors.

"Oh, it was great. Stuffed myself silly, as usual," she laughs before the ringing of the phone interrupts us. "Oh, excuse me. We'll catch up later, okay? Can't wait to hear about Minnesota."

I wave with a smile before venturing into the office space where endless rows of cubicles fill the center and individual offices line the perimeter. My cubicle is in the middle of the fifth row, and I can spot Connor's light-brown hair popping out of the cubicle next to mine before I even round the corner. He pushes back on his chair and swivels it toward me when he spots me approaching, his crooked smile growing, intersecting the oval shape of his face. He's wearing khaki dress shorts and a light-blue button-down shirt, the top button left undone—the only piece of his appearance that isn't perfectly polished and poised. My chest warms at the sight of my friend, and I realize how much I've missed his company while I was gone.

"Hey. You made it back. And you, in fact, did not freeze into a human icicle like you thought." His smile grows even wider, further accentuating the strong line of his jaw, and his olive-green eyes light up simultaneously. Connor has been my cubicle-mate for a few years now, and over that time, we've developed an easy and comfortable work friendship. He's easy to get along with, and we bonded early over our disdain for a few of the less-than-kind realtors that we work with.

"It was close. Any longer and it would have happened. I'm telling you, it was cold," I say with a sigh, dropping my purse onto my desk and sliding into my chair. "It's definitely nice to be back. Has anyone said anything yet? About Makana Manor?"

"Beth says she's going to take a crack at it, but I haven't heard from anyone else," he replies.

"I want it, Connor. I want it bad," I mumble, firing up my laptop and taking a notepad and pen out of my drawer.

"I figured you would," he chuckles as he scratches a spot just above his ear, a pen dangling between two fingers.

"I'm assuming you do too?"

Connor and I are two of the top realtors in the firm, and we're used to working on the same type of high-caliber listings, often consulting with each other when it comes to referrals and helping each other find the perfect listings for our clients.

"I do," he confirms with a strong nod. He looks like he's about to say something else, but he's interrupted.

"Swanson. Brooks," Rich, the other top realtor—one of the less-than-kind ones—booms in greeting as he leans over the top of Connor's cubicle.

"Rich," Connor responds flatly.

"You two aren't vying for the big listing, are you? Wouldn't waste your time on that if I were you," he says smugly.

"We just might. Gotta give you some kind of competition, right?" I say, throwing him a smile that doesn't have an ounce of sincerity behind it.

He snorts, cocking a bushy eyebrow up. "It would be fun to see you try. We all know that listing is not going to be sold by any agent other than me."

His arrogance makes me nauseated, and I swallow down a nasty comeback that threatens to escape. Being professional and courteous in every aspect of my life is important to me, even though Rich tests that resolve nearly every day.

"We'll see," I say sweetly with another forced smile as he laughs and saunters away. "Ugh. He is so…"

"Rude? Arrogant? The owner of annoyingly perfect hair?" Connor quips as he watches Rich walk away.

"Yes," I huff a laugh, "all of the above. He's just so smug about it. I would love nothing more than for someone else to sell this house just to see the look on his face."

Connor swivels his chair once more toward me, pinning me with an intense look that I'm not sure I've seen before. "So I've been thinking…and I have an idea."

"Why does that make me nervous?" I ask hesitantly.

"Why don't we tag team? You and me?" he spits out, raising his brows expectantly.

"Team up?" The surprise in my voice is hardly hidden as I process what he's saying.

He nods, and I can practically see the wheels turning in his head. "Think about it. We all know it's way overpriced—everyone knows that—and not selling it hasn't been for a lack of trying on Brad's part. I've seen the effort he's put into it already. It's a tough sell, for sure. But if we pool our resources and clientele, I think we'd maybe actually have a shot. We could split the commission and bonus."

I admit, it does sound intriguing. I normally like working by myself, but if I were to work with anyone, I would prefer it to be him. I bet we could come up with some creative marketing ideas by brainstorming together, and appealing to both of our large client bases would mean increased odds of finding an actual buyer.

"Two brains are better than one," I say hesitantly, but any doubts I may have had are already quickly dissipating.

"That's what I've always been told," he replies quickly.

I roll my lips and then nod at him with a confident smile. "Okay, let's do it."

"Yeah?" One corner of his mouth pulls up into a lopsided grin.

"Yeah. I mean, we already know we work well with each other. The odds are definitely better if we tackle this thing together," I say.

"That's what I was thinking."

"We'll need a plan, of course." I tap the tip of my pen lightly against my desk, my brain already running in a million different directions.

"Like any solid duo does," he agrees. "I'll be the Robin to your Batman. We'll save the world, one mansion at a time."

"Okay," I laugh, "it's settled, then. Should we plan to meet at the diner tomorrow morning to figure out our strategy? Talking away from the office might be a good idea. You know how these walls tend to talk."

"Absolutely," he says with a final smirk and a determined nod.

3

CONNOR

"Sorry I'm late," Tori says a little breathlessly as she slides into the booth across from me at the local diner near the office. Although it's a Sunday, we're both in our typical business-casual attire—her in a navy-blue tank dress and me in shorts and a sage-green, short-sleeve, button-up shirt.

"I was closing a deal from the parking lot," she explains. Her easy smile lifts her high cheekbones, and she bites at a corner of her full lips at the same time, as if she's trying to keep it from growing too big.

"No problem," I mumble, taking a sip of the fresh black coffee in front of me, feeling the sting of my lip burning a little bit at the contact. "Everything go okay?"

"Yes. There was a lot of back and forth on price during negotiations, but after using what can only be described as my exquisite charm and superb talent, it's ultimately ending with a happy seller and a happy buyer—so that makes for a happy agent." She tucks a strand of her thick wavy hair behind her ear.

Her joy is all-encompassing, luring a slow grin out of me. I always enjoy seeing this side of her—when she's almost giddy with excitement at closing a deal. "Atta girl. I've been on the other end of that charm a time or two in negotiations, so I know its effects. Congratulations."

She gets comfortable in her seat, and I grab for the water pitcher to pour her a glass. For as frequently as we see each other at the office, it's not often that we meet up outside of it—aside from the occasional times when we've met at a property or to negotiate a deal, of course. This will be our first time actually co-listing on a property. Not that I'm complaining. I've always liked being around Tori. There's been a sense of comfort ever since the very first time we met several years ago, which is admittedly not the case with most women I come across in my day-to-day life, and will hopefully bode well for the listing.

"More coffee?" the waitress stops at our booth and asks, offering up the ivory-colored coffee carafe in the direction of my mug.

"Sure. Thanks," I reply, even though my mug is still almost full. I don't miss how her dark eyes stay on mine for an extra beat before focusing on the hot beverage she's pouring. Her long, deep-brown hair falls off one shoulder and cascades down the front of her light-blue apron. She's a beautiful woman, no question about it, but I shift my gaze away from her, suddenly noticing the tell-tale signs of my discomfort. I start to feel fidgety and uneasy, and it's a tad more difficult to breathe.

"Do you need menus?" She directs the question at me, not even bothering to acknowledge Tori, who I can see, out of the corner of my eye, watching us with an amused expression.

"Please." I dip my head in a polite nod before gesturing to Tori to take some of the focus off me. "And Tori? Coffee?"

"Sure," she says with a sly smile. It's only after the waitress disappears to grab menus that Tori lets her grin grow wild, her deep-blue eyes beaming.

"Oh, she practically slid right onto your lap." She smirks.

"Oh, stop." I brush her off, feeling the back of my neck heat up.

"She's pretty. You should totally go for it," Tori urges.

Sweat starts forming on my forehead, and my hands all of a sudden feel clammy. This is the absolute last topic I want to get into right now.

"Nah." I do my best to appear unbothered and unaffected, but I'm not sure how well I'm doing.

"Why not? Are you dating someone? You know, for how good of work friends we are, I know surprisingly very little about your personal life."

I shrug. "Nope, I'm not dating anyone."

"By choice or by circumstance?" she pries, leaning forward. "Oh, she's coming back. Want me to say something? Talk you up?"

"Don't you dare." I glare at her in desperation. My gaze shifts to the front door of the cafe, and I briefly consider making a run for it.

"Here are your menus and a coffee. I'll give you a few minutes." She smiles at me, sweet at first, and then a flirtatious smirk starts to emerge, all in the span of two seconds. I purse my lips together and nod awkwardly despite my best efforts to appear calm and collected.

"Oh my gosh, does she make you nervous?" Tori muses when we're alone again. "This is so cute. You've never struck me as the insecure type."

"I'm not nervous," I insist, wondering how obvious the blatant lie is.

"You look nervous."

"I just…stumble sometimes when talking to women," I admit, the words tumbling out of my mouth. Although, I have no idea why I'm admitting this embarrassing aspect of mine out loud. It's not exactly a fact that I'm proud of.

The truth is, I've just never put a lot of effort into women and dating. I've been career driven and hungry for success since I was a teenager, choosing instead to focus all my efforts on school and then eventually work. Climbing the professional ladder has been my goal for most of my life. I haven't left myself much time for relationships, and for whatever reason, the idea of dating makes me anxious.

"Who would have thought? Real estate powerhouse, Connor Brooks—A shark in business, but no game with the ladies," she teases playfully.

"Alright, enough about me." I roll my eyes, more than ready to move on. "Let's talk about Makana Manor."

"Sorry, you know I'm just teasing." She smiles warmly before curiosity flashes across her face. "But wait. Okay, I'm not done. This doesn't make any sense. You talk to me just fine. In fact, you have no problem whatsoever subjecting me to your dazzling, sarcastic personality."

"You're different," I say simply to the top of my coffee mug, a split second before pressing it to my lips.

"Why is that? Should I be offended?" she scoffs, placing her fingers at her collarbone.

I sigh, realizing I'm not done with this particular conversation yet, despite my efforts to redirect it. "Okay, no offense, but…while you are beautiful…"

She smiles at that, pleased with my choice of wording.

"I've always just looked at you as a coworker and a friend," I say bluntly. "I don't like the idea of dating someone I work with —never have. That's completely off the table. My work life is focused and professional, and I don't want to mix any kind of relationship into it. So it's easy to talk to you because there's no potential of something more. The pressure is off. Does that make sense?"

"It does." She shrugs, contemplating what I said before eventually nodding in agreement.

"Are we done now? Can we move on from analyzing my non-existent dating life?"

"Sure," she concedes with a smile.

"Alright, so Makana Manor…I've already started compiling my list of high-end clientele from overseas that might be interested in a vacation home here," I start.

"Same," she agrees, growing serious. "My virtual Rolodex is filled with potential buyers that are out of state. I think focusing on the appeal of a luxury vacation home in paradise is a good strategy for this one. I mean, it's the ultimate slice of heaven—to anyone who can afford it, that is. As far as locals, we should obviously do some open houses? Maybe an event?"

"That's a good idea," I agree. "Did Brad say there were any stipulations from the homeowner, Steve? Any restrictions on open houses, accessing the house, or anything like that?"

Tori pulls a manila folder out of her laptop case and sets it on the table in front of her, moving the menu to the side. She pulls out a stack of papers and starts thumbing through them.

"Here we go." She scans the paper and then shakes her head. "Nope. In fact, Mr. Sherwood is not even living there at the moment. We can have access to the property at any time. There's a lockbox on the front door, and the code to get in is right here, as well as the code to get past the private gate."

"Perfect." Anticipation starts buzzing just under my skin. I absolutely love this part of my job. Of strategizing and coming up with creative ways to showcase a house, especially a challenging, over-priced one, to eventually find the perfect buyer and get the house under contract. The challenge of it all fuels me.

"I brought you a cinnamon-streusel muffin. On the house." The waitress slides the muffin in front of me with a wink before pulling out her notepad. "Now, what can I get you?" She looks expectantly at me.

I clear my throat, feeling uncomfortable again under her unrelenting stare. "I'll do eggs, over-easy, and hash browns with a side of toast, please."

"Great choice. And for your…girlfriend?" She swings her eyes over to Tori, who's pushing her lips together in an attempt to not smile.

"Friend," Tori happily offers, and I mentally roll my eyes. "I'll have an everything omelet, please. And a side of toast as well."

"You got it. I'll be back." She grabs our menus and walks away with a renewed pep in her step.

"Here," I say, sliding the muffin to the center of the table.

"That muffin is not for me," Tori says pointedly, holding back a laugh.

"Stop being childish and have half of this muffin," I say, then continue on in an attempt to return to our conversation before more teasing begins. "I think we should go look at the house. I've never seen the inside of it in person, only the listing photos."

"I haven't either. That's a great idea. Maybe it'll spark some more ideas for us too."

"I have a few showings on other properties this afternoon, but tomorrow morning is free for me. Do you want to meet then?" I ask.

"Yes, that works for me. I want to get the ball rolling on this ASAP so we can get a good handle on it. Nothing would devastate me more than losing this listing to Rich." Her mouth turns up, and she sticks the tip of her tongue out in disgust.

I chuckle. "I can think of several other devastating things, but I get your point."

"Plus, the commission and bonus on this property is absolutely insane. It would be the biggest sale of my career."

"Same," I agree emphatically. Although, if I'm honest, the

status of selling this house and what that would mean for furthering my career means more to me than the earning potential. The idea of being the realtor who sold it—even alongside Tori—is so intoxicating to me that it never strays far from my mind throughout our breakfast and the entire rest of my day.

4

TORI

In the parking lot of the diner, I sit in my white MINI Cooper convertible with my laptop propped on the center console to respond back to the eleven emails that filled my inbox while I was inside with Connor. Even though it is the weekend—and a holiday one, at that—real estate doesn't pause on Saturdays and Sundays. In fact, with the nature of the business, it's often busier on these days than the actual workweek.

I finish up and click out of my last email, powering my laptop off. One of the things I like the most about real estate is the fact that I'm not glued to an office chair for eight hours a day. I'm constantly running between properties, meeting clients at various locations to discuss listings, putting offers together to submit, or answering emails from anywhere. There's spontaneity and fluidity in my workday, which I love and am so thankful for. However, it also means that it can be hard to turn off.

Admittedly, I often get sucked into the rabbit hole that is my phone, no matter where I go.

After putting everything away, I start heading over to my parents' house, where all my siblings and their families are gathering for our weekly Sunday afternoon lunch. I keep the radio off, choosing instead to savor the silence. I learned a long time ago that in order to save my sanity before family gatherings, I need to ground myself and soak up some calm before the inevitable chaos ensues. I love my siblings and am, of course, an active participant in the mayhem, but it can get to be a lot sometimes.

The road runs right along a quiet stretch of beach. It's pretty sparse, people-wise, compared to other touristy beaches on the island that are always jam-packed with bodies. There are just a few people that I can see out my car window—one couple holding hands as they walk along the shoreline, and another woman farther back from the shore, lying on a beach towel with a floppy straw hat on top of her face and an open book resting across her chest. A pang of jealousy hits, and I make a mental note to carve out some time soon to lounge on the beach.

When I approach the brightly colored ice cream shop on the corner of the intersection, I turn right to continue on the road that leads to my parents' house. I don't bother knocking when I arrive and push my way through the front door, where I'm immediately enveloped by a chorus of voices—some big, some small—that fill the house as I make my way up the stairs.

"Tori!" my niece, Lily, shouts in greeting as she runs past me down the hallway.

"Hi, Lily-bear." I smile as I make my way into the kitchen, where my siblings, my mom, and Paige are all gathered around the island.

"Tori, weigh in on this for us, please," my sister, Grace, who's leaning against the counter, says to me in lieu of an official greeting. "Emily and Scott are thinking of spending the morning of their wedding together. Waking up with each other, getting coffee and all that, before separating to get ready for the ceremony. What do you think? I personally think it's bad luck."

"It's totally bad luck," my sister, Ava, Lily's mom, pipes in before I can answer. "Plus, it's tradition. The groom is not supposed to see the bride on the day of the wedding until their first look."

"Screw tradition. We live together, for Pete's sake. Who cares?" Emily says in exasperation.

"Well, I think you already know my vote on this one," Mom jumps in before looking at me for backup.

"I think you should do whatever you and Scott want to do," I say to Emily with a wink before wincing apologetically at my mom. I grab a slice of pepper jack cheese from the appetizer platter that's centered on the counter and take a bite.

"Of course, you would say that," Ava says. "You haven't been married. Do you really want to start your married life off with bad luck? Matt, what do you think?"

From the corner, Matt's head jerks up at the sound of his name as if he had been tuning us out. He swallows the cracker he had just popped in his mouth and looks square at Emily with an expressionless stare. "I mean this in the most loving way possible, Emily… I literally could not care less."

I snicker as his remark causes eye rolls and scoffs from around the room like it's offensive that he isn't as invested in the topic as they are. Matt shrugs and makes his way to the living room, where I assume Dad and the brothers-in-law are watching football.

"I say we take a break from the wedding talk," Ava, Emily's matron of honor, says. "We'll circle back after we eat and everyone is a little less hangry and opinionated."

"Good idea," Grace says, turning her attention on me. "Tori, how's your love life? Did you meet any burly Minnesotan men while you were there?"

"Sadly, no," I chuckle. Being the youngest of us four kids and the only one not currently engaged or married, I'm used to taking these dating questions in stride. Unfortunately, there hasn't been much to share recently. Work has been keeping me way too busy to date. Not to mention that all of the eligible, decent men on this island are few and far between, and apparently, I attract the complete opposite—emotionally or physically unavailable men, most of the time both. After a long string of terrible, underwhelming dates, I've been putting dating on the back-burner for the last little while.

"Can you imagine? A bearded, muscular, flannel-loving man who you just know would be able to keep you alive in any inclement weather?" Emily asks dreamily.

"Sign me up," Ava quips.

"So, how was your Thanksgiving? We missed you guys," Mom says to me, ignoring the outwardly objectifying conversation happening around her while she slides a plate of freshly baked cookies toward me. Boisterous shouting erupts from the living room, that I can only assume is aimed at the television.

"It was great," I tell her, taking a cookie. "We had a lot of fun. I did fly home a day early, though. There's a big listing at work that's up for grabs—along with a bonus if it sells. Connor and I are teaming up to try and sell it."

"Is he the cute one?" Grace lights up.

"There's a cute one?" Ava asks.

"Stop." I shrug them off nonchalantly with a crease of my brows. "He's my work friend."

"Your cute work friend, if I remember correctly." Grace has been with me a time or two when I've needed to swing by the office to grab something, so she's well aware of who Connor is.

"Oh, do tell." Paige rests her elbow on the counter and then her chin in her hand.

"There's nothing to tell," I say firmly, feeling protective of my friendship with him and not wanting to gossip any more on the topic. "Unlike some people"—I grab a bottle of water from the fridge and point it toward Emily—"I keep my work life professional." She rolls her eyes at my jab toward her and Scott, who just so happens to be not only her fiancé but also her boss.

Baring my teeth in an overly cheesy smile, I make my escape by walking around to the sliding door that leads to the deck. I slip out into the humid air and down to the backyard, where I just spotted Elliot reading under a palm tree.

"Hey, there's my favorite nephew," I say, crossing the yard to have a seat next to him in the shade.

"I'm your only nephew," he points out.

"True. But you're still my favorite." I nudge his shoulder.

"I feel like I might have too many aunts to say you're my favorite…right?" He peers at me through his glasses.

"That's okay," I laugh. "We both know it's true. What are you reading?"

"*The Dragon Encyclopedia*." He flips the thick book closed to show me the cover. "It has everything that I'll ever need to know about dragons."

"Wow. That is a lot of information." A gust of wind brushes by, making the strap of my tank top fall off my shoulder. "School starts again tomorrow, right? Are you ready to go back?"

"I guess. I wish we could have stayed in Minnesota a little bit longer, though. It's just so different here. I miss all of the things you can only do in the cold weather."

"Yeah…I'm pretty sure we would melt on the spot if we drank some hot chocolate right now." My skin is starting to feel clammy from being out in this heat, and it hasn't even been five minutes.

"Probably," he agrees with a sad laugh.

"I'll tell you what. How about sometime this week, I'll take you to the beach, and we'll try to make a sandman?" I offer.

"Really?" He lights up.

"Sure. I bet we could make a pretty nice little family out of sand. I don't think anything will beat your snowmen family, but we can sure try."

"Okay." He nods with an excited smile.

"Okay. It's a date. Now let's head inside and see what Grandma made for lunch, shall we?" I offer him a hand to help him up, and with books and art supplies under our arms, we head back toward the house.

$$5$$

$$\rule{120px}{1px}$$

CONNOR

"Good morning, Mr. Brooks," Ruth calls from the couch that's nestled in the entryway of my grandparents' assisted living building. Without fail, this sweet old lady is the first person I see every single time I'm buzzed through the front doors. I've discovered she's not only a creature of habit but a social butterfly. She moseys on down to this sitting area every morning after her breakfast and spends almost the entire rest of her day greeting everyone who walks by.

The sitting area that she's in is off to the right, while the front office and hallway to the kitchen are immediately on the left. I give a nod to the gentlemen behind the desk and keep venturing into the building.

"Good morning, Ruth." I give her a friendly smile and wave as I make my way past her to the elevators. I've learned that it's best to keep moving. Otherwise, I'll get sucked into a never-ending story of the latest gossip and drama that fills the walls of this place —all of which I have absolutely zero time for or interest in if I'm being honest. I involuntarily shiver as I step onto the elevator, the cool temperature of the air conditioning already giving me a chill.

"Tell your grandmother she still owes me five dollars from the gin rummy match yesterday…" Ruth's voice trails off as the elevator door starts to close, but not before I throw her another curt wave and smile, not wanting to be rude.

On the third floor, I hook a left and follow the faint thumping music down the hall as it gradually gets louder, unsurprised to discover that it's coming from their unit. I shift the grocery bag into my other hand, then knock twice before opening the door and letting myself in, the music piercing my ears as the door opens.

"Hello?" I call out, pulling the door shut behind me.

"Connor? Is that you?" my grandma, Betty, calls from the kitchen area that's on the other side of the wall to the left.

"It's me, Grandma." I round the corner to find her sitting at the kitchen table across from my grandpa Lou. Both of their faces light up when they spot me.

"Connor, sweetie! Louie, turn the music down." Grandma waves in the direction of the remote. My grandpa startles and lifts his shoulders in surprise, as if he just noticed the volume, then fumbles the remote in his hands, searching for the right button.

"One second, here…" he mumbles, pulling his glasses farther down on his nose.

"Oh, for Pete's sake, Louie, turn it down." She glares at him. I bite back a laugh when the volume gets louder, and Grandma lifts her arms in annoyed defeat.

"I got it," I say with a smile, gently taking the remote from his hands. I pat his shoulder reassuringly once the music reaches a comfortable level. "Technology these days, huh?"

"You truly can't figure these remotes out," he huffs in agreement. "Way too many damn buttons."

"Completely unnecessary." I shake my head in solidarity.

"Come here, my boy." Grandma stands up, and I meet her for a hug before setting the grocery bag on the table and sliding into a chair. "What can I get you? Coffee? Some tea? Pie? Your grandfather hasn't eaten all of the Thanksgiving leftovers yet."

"Oh, I'm fine. I can't stay long." I don't know why I bother protesting, as she's already fumbling through the cabinets for a glass. "I just wanted to drop off some fresh produce before I head off to work."

"Oh, thank you, dear. You didn't need to do that, you know," she says.

My parents live on the Big Island, and while they're close enough to check in on my grandparents often, as the sole grandchild, I take it upon myself to drop by at least weekly and am often their go-to person if they need help with anything. Dropping off groceries when I can is the least I can do. Grandma decides on a glass of orange juice and places it in front of me before pulling the contents out of the bag.

"Bananas. Oh, look, Louie—pineapple! Your favorite."

"Bless your heart, boy," my grandpa says. "Did you remember to—"

"I already cut it up," I interject, which earns me a smile and a pat on my forearm.

"For some reason, Betty doesn't trust me with knives anymore," he grumbles.

"Louie, we're ninety-three years old. I don't trust you with a hairbrush these days," she retorts.

"Alright, alright." My phone buzzes in my pocket, and it's a knee-jerk reaction to pull it out and see who's calling. I stand up, gulp down the juice in one shot, and give them each a kiss on the cheek. "I've gotta head out. Call me if you need anything, okay?"

"Ah, we're just fine. Look, that was a whole six minutes. I think that's a record for you!" Grandpa says.

"One of these days I'll stay for a longer visit, but you know…"

"Work calls. We know. Thank you for stopping by. It's always good to see you, you know," Grandma says, following me to the door.

"Anytime." With one last smile, I pull the door shut behind me. I return the phone call to my client as I make my way back down the elevator, ending the call shortly after the doors open. In the lobby, I luckily manage to sneak past Ruth, who's deep in conversation with another woman, and head out the front doors. Heat rolls over me as I step outside, making the goosebumps on my arms vanish within seconds.

As soon as I settle in my gray Tesla, I roll the windows down, check my work email on my phone one more time, and then head out of the parking lot. I drive down the palm-tree-lined road that weaves through the neighborhood surrounding my grandparents' building and through the surrounding streets of Honolulu. I slide my sunglasses on just as I make a turn, and a beam of sunshine glares off my windshield. I slow down to let a group of kids riding their bikes cross to the other side of the street. The neighborhood is bustling with people walking on the sidewalk or standing in small groups in the middle of driveways, casually catching up with their neighbors. In the twenty minutes it takes to drive to Kailua Beach, I've mentally scanned through my various open listings and my to-do list for each of them in my mind, including confirming the inspection that's scheduled at the inland single-family home one of my clients is purchasing, and returning Trish's call at the title office.

As I turn down a side road and approach the entrance gate all the way at the end of the street, I punch the code into the keypad that's built into the post. When the gates open, I circle the winding driveway that runs along the front of the sprawling ten-thousand-square-foot estate that already screams luxury just by the look of the front.

I park behind Tori's car, then climb up the sprawling concrete staircase that leads to two massive columns and a spacious front porch. After taking a minute to admire the immaculate landscaping that flanks the stairs, I let myself in the front door. I'm greeted by high ceilings, a spacious open area, and a grand spiral staircase to the right.

"Hey! In here," Tori calls from the kitchen. My loafers gently tap against the tile floor and echo off the high ceilings as I make my way straight ahead through the large entryway. I find her in a light-blue halter sundress and heels, eyes glued to her phone, and perched on a barstool that's tucked under the kitchen island. A pile of papers is loosely stacked next to her open laptop. Her hair is pulled off to one side, hanging in front of her right shoulder.

"Look at you—right at home," I say in greeting.

"I'm manifesting." She smirks, setting her phone down. "I can really envision myself here."

"Naturally. This place is insane." Roaming around the marble island, I take note of the light-wood cabinets of the kitchen, stainless steel high-end appliances, two beverage fridges, and built-in wine rack. Tucked in the corner is a large, walk-in, climate-controlled pantry, complete with its own sink and microwave.

With a whistle, I meander past the wooden dining table that sits under an opulent pendant light fixture and over to the living area that has a leather sofa, two chairs, and a coffee table that's all nestled in front of a fireplace. What I guess to be a seventy-five-inch television hangs above the mantel.

I peek down a hallway to the left of the fireplace that I know has a bathroom, laundry room, and garage access, judging by what the listing details online said. Roaming back around, I notice the floor-to-ceiling retractable sliding doors in between the living room and dining table, that leads outside to an outdoor dining area on the vast patio and a large infinity pool.

"Look at this place," I breathe, making my way back to the kitchen island.

"I know, right?" Tori slides off the stool. "I got here a little early and explored. Come on. I'll show you around."

6

—————

TORI

"Check this out. There's an elevator," I say, opening the door to point inside. "You won't catch me dead in here, but if you want to try it out, I can meet you upstairs."

"What, you don't like small spaces?" Connor asks, poking his head inside, inspecting every corner of the small, boxy machine.

"Call me crazy, but I just don't like the potential of it getting stuck while I'm halfway up. The possibility of being stranded somewhere inside these walls with no one around to hear my screams…no, thank you."

"I'd save you," he says nonchalantly, his eyes continuing their scan of every square inch of this place before pinning me with a mischievous grin. "It would make for a great ghost story, though, if you ended up dying in there."

I roll my eyes playfully. "The good news is, we'll never know. Come on. I haven't seen the upstairs yet, either."

We continue past the elevator to where the back staircase is, and we head up the stairs. I run my hand softly along the black steel railing in admiration until we reach the top. This estate has eight bedrooms in total, and we take our time exploring the seven that are in the right wing—all similarly designed with coastal-chic décor, top-of-the-line furnishings, and each with their own pristine white ensuite bathrooms—until we reach the primary bedroom in the left wing.

"This view," I gasp, heading straight past the lush California-king bed to the sliding doors that lead out to the balcony.

"Buyers are absolutely going to love this." Connor comes next to me, resting a hand against the ledge that overlooks the pool below. There are two rows of lounge chairs on each side of the pool and a separate pool house off to the right side. Beyond the edge of the infinity pool, you can see the one-hundred-twenty-three-foot stretch of private beach and the clear blue of the vast rolling ocean behind it. Large palm trees flank both sides of the house, creating a cozy, lush-green canopy that hugs the structure tightly.

"Breathtaking. As beautiful as this is, I'm dying to see what every woman will be longing to see—" I start retreating back into the room.

"The separate toilets?" Connor cuts in, trailing behind me.

"The closets, duh." I head down a short hallway to the right of the room and open the first door that leads to a massive walk-in closet. Floor-to-ceiling custom white cabinets and display cases line the perimeter of the room while a large island sits in the middle, a small chandelier hovering over the top. A cushioned bench sits along the forefront of the island, and a floor-length mirror is tucked in the corner. It seems that every small detail has been thought through, including a hanger wall for purses, a drawer specifically made to organize watches, and a display case solely for sunglasses. My mouth drops open involuntarily as I scan the shoe display that runs four shelves wide.

"Here, you got a little…drool, right there…" Connor teases, touching the corner of his lip.

"Shut up," I laugh breathily. "I've seen—and sold—some very impressive homes with very nice closets in my day, but this one definitely takes the cake."

"It is impressive. I'll give you that." Connor pulls out a drawer that perfectly houses rows of organized baseball hats.

"Alright, I might not ever leave if I stay in here any longer," I say. "Let's check out the bathroom." I gaze longingly one more time at the space before shutting off the dimmer switches and closing the closet door behind me.

"Now this is what I'm talking about," Connor mutters as we enter the bathroom, stepping onto the marble tile. He heads straight for the walk-in shower that has multiple shower heads coming out of the wall at several different angles and even an overhead rain shower option. I run my fingertips along the matte gray cabinets that have black hardware and the white marble countertops with the double sink. Small beachy accents and greenery are peppered throughout the bathroom, adding to the modern yet coastal vibe.

"Oh my gosh," I breathe, approaching the standalone white soaking tub that's settled in front of a giant window with a view of the ocean. "Can you imagine if this was your view every night?"

Fueled by a moment of spontaneity, I slip my heels off, set them gently on the tile, and step inside the tub. I smooth my dress down as I sit, crossing my ankles and resting my arms along the outer rim.

"Are you comfortable?" Connor smirks in amusement, coming to hover over me, sliding both of his hands into the pockets of his khaki shorts.

"Very," I whisper, leaning my head back so it rests against

the ledge and closing my eyes. "All I need is a glass of wine and a good book. Maybe some soft music."

"Move over."

My eyes snap open just in time to see Connor stepping into the tub. A flash of hesitation flashes across his face, but it disappears completely when he climbs all the way in, nudging my legs out of the way as he lowers himself down.

"What are you doing?" I grumble. "You're ruining my daydream."

"This is nice," he confirms to himself with a nod, ignoring my comment. He tugs on the bottom of his white button-up shirt to smooth it out, and his outstretched legs come to rest beside me, my outer thigh squishing against his. "You can easily fit two people in here."

He looks out the window, completely unfazed by the fact that we're two grown adults—coworkers, at that—crammed together in an empty soaking tub that doesn't belong to either of us.

"This is weird," I point out. Connor swivels his head to meet my gaze.

"It's not weird. We have to get a feel for things if we're expected to sell it, right? Immerse ourselves in it. Get to know it. Get comfortable with the space."

"I'm aware. That's why I got in here in the first place. I just didn't expect you to follow me in," I say with a pointed smirk. He shrugs nonchalantly, his eyebrows pulling up in amusement. His skin looks especially dark and tanned against the white of the tub, and his toned frame fills out his work attire nicely. I don't know when he finds the time to work out, but clearly he does. He is, admittedly, the most attractive man I've ever been in a bathtub with. It's a real shame that this is purely platonic and work-related.

"So, should we talk strategy?" He grows serious, the line on his forehead creasing as his green eyes hold mine. I can feel the tiniest flinch of his leg against mine as he readjusts, and the spot on my thigh where our legs meet flushes with a subtle warmth at the contact.

"Sure." I nod before clearing my throat, shifting my focus away from our touching skin. "Okay, let's run through a checklist. Obviously, Brad already has the listing up with all the info and professional photos, but what do you think about hiring a videographer to come through and put together some sort of fresh virtual tour experience that we can push out in social media blasts and both of our email lists?"

He nods, chewing at the corner of his lip, deep in thought. "I like that. Seeing it in person is definitely what's going to sell this house. The pictures don't do it justice, so I think you're right. A virtual experience is the next best thing for out-of-state buyers."

I gaze out the window at the horizon above the ocean and get lost in a brainstorming fog, feeling perhaps more comfortable than I should be as I'm lazily pressed against him.

"And definitely some type of open house for the locals," Connor breaks the silence. "But we have to get creative with that one—Brad's already done several this past year with no luck."

Nodding my head, I look around the bathroom, scanning all of the small details, until an idea sparks. I sit up slightly, feeling a twinge of excitement. "Okay, hear me out…we're coming up on December, right? We're about to sink deep into the holiday season. Can you imagine this place at Christmastime? How absolutely stunning and magical it is? What if we host an open house but make it a fancy holiday black-tie gala?"

"Oh, I like that." His eyes perk up, piercing mine as excitement of his own builds behind them.

"We could go to the tree farm and pick out a tree," I say, the ideas that are flooding my mind out loud. "Get stockings, decorations, hire a catering company, all of it—really go all out with the aesthetic and show agents and potential buyers the kind of upscale holiday party that you could throw here."

"Yes. I love it. We'll have to do it relatively soon. We don't want to cut it too close. It needs to be under contract by the thirty-first in order to win," he points out.

I glance at the calendar on my Apple watch. "How about in about two weeks? December 15th? Do you think we can get it all done in such a short amount of time?"

"We can do it. Just get ready to see a lot of me in the next couple of weeks." He says it in a way that makes me question whether it's meant to be a threat or a dare.

"I don't know if I can handle that," I tease. "But I can suck it up for the cause. First thing is coming up with a guest list and then creating and sending out invitations so people can get the date on their calendars."

"We should probably get out of this tub, then, huh?" he asks after a brief moment of silence.

"Probably a good idea. Let's head to the office and get started," I say excitedly as he climbs out and reaches back to offer a hand and help me out of the bathtub.

7

———————

TORI

With a sigh, I finally slide out of my heels and drop my laptop bag gently on the floor next to my front door. There's nothing quite like coming home to my quiet condo at the end of a long, busy day. My own calm little sanctuary that's ready and waiting for me to relax into and finally let my guard down. The stress and bustle of the day always start to dissipate the moment I walk through my front door.

First things first, I grab myself a wine glass, choose a bottle of chardonnay from the wine rack, and pour some into the glass. After a quick sip, I pull ingredients out of the fridge to put together a chicken Caesar salad. As I make myself a salad bowl, my mind drifts to the workday and everything that we ended up accomplishing.

After meeting Connor at Makana Manor, we met back at the office and got started compiling a master guest list for the gala. We added all the agents on the islands that we know who might have interested clients, as well as several of our own high-end clients from around the world. Besides needing to pause once when I ran to show another client of mine a potential house and then again when Connor spent almost an entire hour on a phone call, we spent the rest of the day together, designing and perfecting the invitation we plan to send out soon.

Now that I'm at home, I feel a sense of fatigue start to spread deep in my bones. Grabbing my wine glass, the salad, and the pile of today's mail, I pass through the living room and open the sliding door that leads to my balcony. Balancing everything in my arms, I manage to grab my favorite cozy knit blanket from the basket by the door and settle onto one of my wicker-rattan lounge chairs that has a thick white cushion across the top.

This time of year often brings a slight chill in the evening air, so I stretch the blanket all the way over my bent knees and tuck it around my toes. As I eat, I admire the view in front of me. The community swimming pool is visible down below, with incandescent pool lights illuminating the perimeter of the pool and the connected hot tub. White twinkling Christmas lights are strung along the row of palm trees that surround the outdoor area, and between them is the tiny view of the beach and ocean that juts up to the pool area.

The sun continues its descent as I relax and eat the rest of my meal. A gust of wind rolls through my hair, and I can practically taste the salt from the ocean on my tongue. I set the salad bowl down to curl the blanket up higher until it rests just below my chin. After a few solitary moments of soaking in the quiet and several sips of wine, I start sifting through the pile of mail.

I excitedly pick out the ones that look like Christmas cards and open the first one which ends up being from my best friend, Quinn, and her fiancé, Brian. The card reads *Merry Christmas with lots of love, Brian and Quinn.* Below is a picture of them with their arms around each other in front of the Eiffel Tower. Quinn is a travel photographer and is often away from Oahu, gallivanting around the world and chasing adventures. This picture was from a recent trip to France that she took with Brian. With a smile, I remind myself to call her tomorrow to check in. She's gone so much, and we don't see each other often, but we still try to stay connected as best we can through frequent phone chats.

The second card has a return address of St. Petersburg, Florida. I slide the card out, revealing a picture of a family grouped together in front of the Salvador Dali Museum.

Another one?

Confused, I flip the card over to the inscription that reads *May this Christmas season bring only happiness and joy to you and your family. Love, The Baxters.*

"I don't understand," I mumble to myself. Once again, I have no idea who the Baxters are and why they would have sent me a card. My name and address must have gotten mixed up with someone else's somewhere—I don't know. It doesn't make any sense. Receiving one card could have been a fluke, but now that there have been two? Something doesn't seem quite right. With a shake of my head, I tear open and go through the rest of the mail before setting it off to the side and nestling back against the cushion.

Aside from the slight echoing from the voices of a couple taking an evening dip in the pool below and the rustling of the palm trees, the air is tranquil and peaceful. I spend the next half-hour watching the sun finish setting until the chill in the air gets to be too much, and I head inside to get ready for bed.

"This looks nothing like a snowman," Elliot says quietly, assessing the sorry excuse for a sandman that we've spent the last hour building. The lopsided sand fixture crumbles apart, with sand cascading down the right side, landing in a heap next to it.

"I know," I say, wiping my damp forehead with my forearm. "I think we need to rethink our strategy here. Obviously, this isn't working."

"We need more water," Matt says confidently, grabbing the bucket before walking to the shore to scoop up some more ocean water.

You can't do anything in this family without it spreading like wildfire, so when I asked Elliot if he wanted to come to the beach after work today to build a sandman, it was no surprise that we had a few extra helpers—aka my siblings—randomly show up to help.

"Maybe we should try rolling the ball in the sand like you do with snow," Paige suggests from where she's sitting on a blanket off to the side with Noelle.

"It might just be too big. A smaller one might work," Ava says.

"Maybe everyone needs to grab a spot and hold it in place until it forms," Emily adds, standing and placing her hand on her hip.

"Because we have all evening." Grace rolls her eyes. "I say we call it a day and relax with a margarita instead."

Seemingly ignoring all the suggestions, Elliot gets back to work gathering sand to start fresh. "Here," I say, brushing the sand off of my jean shorts and helping Elliot bring the bucket of sand to where Matt set the bucket of water. "Let's try this again, huh?"

We grab a small handful of sand, add lots of water, forming it into a round, sticky ball. We add a little bit more, adding it slower than we did the last time. Little by little, we manage to roll a large enough ball for the base of the sandman, and surprisingly, it isn't falling apart.

"See? I told you making it smaller would work," Ava says smugly.

"You had absolutely nothing to do with the fact that this was successful," Emily laughs. "You hardly lifted a finger. Let's not pretend like you were an active participant over there on your beach towel."

"But who's the one that's all sandy and out of breath? 'Cause it's definitely not me," Ava says with a teasing smile.

Tuning them out, I focus on the task at hand. The next hour is spent constructing two more sand balls and ever so carefully placing them on top of each other, creating the best version of a sandman that we possibly can. Elliot grabs three rocks and carefully places them down the middle ball to serve as the buttons, then he runs to rummage through the beach bag. I put two seashells in place for the eyes, and then Elliot hands me a pair of sunglasses to place over them.

"Can't forget the Santa hat," Elliot says excitedly, setting it on top of the sandman. "It is Christmastime, after all."

"That it is." I smile. "Now it's just missing some arms. Should we look for some sticks?"

A few of us walk the shoreline, the ocean water splashing over our feet as it comes in waves, while some search under nearby trees for any stray sticks. Eventually, we come up with a little pile and let Elliot choose which two he wants to use for the arms. When we're all done, we gather next to the sandman while Matt takes a picture of us with our masterpiece.

"I'm actually really impressed with this," I tell Elliot. "It's been a really long time since I've made one of these."

"Thanks for helping me." He squeezes me in a bear hug with a huge smile on his face.

"Absolutely." My phone dings in my pocket with a notification, and I carefully pull it out to see a reminder that I had set. "Actually, that was perfect timing because I have to head out."

"You're leaving? Already?" Emily asks.

"Isn't the work day over by now?" Ava asks.

"The work day is hardly ever over for her. You know that," Grace says.

"This is true," I agree with a smile. "No rest for the successful."

Emily cracks open a hard seltzer from her spot on the sand. "I feel like there was a jab in there somewhere, but I'm too tired to read into it."

"Where are you going?" Paige asks me.

"Connor and I need to go pick out a tree for Makana Manor, and we really want to get that done today. We were supposed to go earlier, but I pushed it back because I absolutely needed to make a sandman today." I ruffle Elliot's hair with a smile.

"Oh, what a cute little date idea—a Christmas tree farm? That's so cliché and adorable," Grace says in an overly sweet voice.

"You know it's not a date," I say pointedly in response.

"Just let me live vicariously through you and believe that you actually are dating your hunky coworker." She waves her hand, dismissing me, pulling her sunglasses down over her eyes.

"Believe what you want. I have to go get cleaned up quick. I'll see you guys later. Elliot…epic job today, buddy! I'm proud of us."

With a quick round of high-fives and hugs, I rush off the beach to get ready to meet up with Connor.

8

———————

CONNOR

"Are you team artificial tree or team real tree?" Tori asks as she runs her hand along a branch of a dense Leyland cypress tree.

Instead of choosing one of the many pre-cut trees that were imported from the mainland and available at various stores around town—as I had suggested—Tori thought that was too easy and wanted to come to this local Christmas tree farm that's just outside of Honolulu. Apparently, they have the best selection, which is evident by the rows of trees that seem to go on for miles. However, I have a sneaking suspicion the signature Christmas Moscow Mule that they offer as a refreshing beverage had something to do with her choosing this place as well.

"Fake tree. Honestly, I usually don't even put a tree up at my place at all," I admit with a shrug.

"Are you serious?" she gasps, looking stricken as if I'd just told her I dislike children. "Don't tell me you're a grinch, and you hate Christmas? Oh no, I don't think we can be friends anymore if that's the case. I won't be able to get past this now that I know you have coal in place of your heart."

"I'm not a grinch." I laugh, leaning in to get a whiff of the light pine scent of a smaller, round tree.

"You just have something against Christmas trees?"

"Not specifically." I crouch down to inspect the trunk and bottom branches of a tree, pretending to actually know what constitutes a good pick. "Listen, I'm the only one who lives in my house, and you know how busy my job keeps me. Most years, I'm lucky if I get a wreath on the front door."

"Ah, yes. I know your type well. I, too, am a fellow workaholic," Tori says, an amusing smile playing on her lips. "At least we own it. But I do make an effort when it comes to Christmas, the most magical time of the year."

"Let me guess, you're a real-tree kind of girl?" A sudden gust of warm air feels especially thick as my black T-shirt starts to stick against my chest. I grip my copper mug and bring the ice-cold ginger-beer-and-vodka cocktail to my mouth, narrowly avoiding a floating cranberry and rosemary sprig. I appreciate the refreshingly cold drink as I take a few sips and feel it travel all the way down my throat, cooling me from the inside out.

"Yes and no. I would absolutely love a real one, but my condo building doesn't allow us to have real trees in our units. Something about fire hazards and disposal complications." She shrugs.

"Valid concerns." My phone vibrates in my pocket, and without thinking, I instantly take it out to scan the three new emails that just hit my inbox. At first glance, there's nothing that needs my immediate attention.

"So I'm forced to have an artificial one. I might put it up this week, actually. Hey! Why don't we get you a real one while we're here?"

"Tonight?" I ask, sliding my phone back into my pocket.

"Yeah! We have Matt's Jeep, so we might as well load one

more on top of it. Come on! I'll help you set it up and everything. We can swing by your house first." She looks adorably giddy with excitement. So much so that it almost makes me want to say yes.

"I'm gonna go with no on that one." The maintenance and upkeep of a real tree makes me wary. Setting it up, only to spend hours decorating it, and then watering it daily, only to take it all down again in a few weeks. Who has time for all that? And for just me to stare at it? What's the point, honestly?

"Let's just see if one jumps out at you," she says, walking ahead, either ignoring or dismissing my refusal.

"How, exactly, does a Christmas tree jump out at you?" I follow behind her, our shoes kicking up little clouds of sand as we walk along the dusty path.

"You'll just feel it. It'll choose you, don't worry." She squeezes between two trees with her hand over the top of her mug, crossing over to the next row.

"Will it, now?" I smirk in amusement, following behind her, needles poking at my arm on the way through.

"So, tell me about your family," she says, starting her inspection of this row as if they all don't look exactly the same. "I don't know much about them."

"Not much to tell. I'm an only child. My parents are on the Big Island. It's just my grandparents and me here on Oahu."

"That's it?" she asks after a brief pause, waiting for me to say more. "No aunts or uncles? Cousins or anything?"

"Not here. My only aunt and uncle live in Michigan, but they never had kids. And my other set of grandparents have already passed away."

"Wow. That seems so small to me."

"You have your brother and at least one sister, right?" I ask, remembering a gal who has stopped by the office a few times to see her.

"Oh, bless your heart," she huffs a laugh. "That's just a

fraction of my family. I have four siblings—Matt and then three sisters—all of whom have significant others. And then there are my parents, two nieces, and a nephew. And that's just my immediate family."

"Can't imagine what your family gatherings look like."

"I'll give you three hints—loud, boisterous, and opinionated."

"You say that so lovingly."

"I love my family." She chuckles. "Therefore, I'm allowed to say that they're insufferable sometimes."

"Hey, knock yourself out if you need to vent. I won't tell on you," I say with a shrug. I'm just about to follow her through to the next row of trees when the toe of my shoe gets caught on a stray branch, sending me stumbling forward. In a split-second attempt to miss plowing straight into Tori, I stumble to the left, face-first into the middle of a tree.

"Pffftt," Tori puffs out a loud laugh, bending over at the waist, her wavy blonde hair falling forward. I can't see her face, but I can hear her squeals and gasps of laughter as I attempt to untangle myself from the tree.

"I'm glad you think this is funny," I say flatly, picking needles out of my shirt and reaching for the now-empty copper mug that had rolled off to the side.

"I'm sorry," she gasps, running a finger under her eye. "But that was amazing. Are you okay?"

"I'm fine," I grumble, feeling slightly embarrassed that Tori witnessed that clumsy moment.

"Hey, you know what?" she asks, bringing her laughing down to a chuckle and coming closer to pull a needle out of my hair.

"Couldn't even try to guess what."

Her eyes are twinkling when she says, "I think this tree just chose you."

"Oh, for Pete's sake." I can't roll my eyes hard enough.

She responds with more giggling. "Should we follow the signs of the universe and get this one for you? I kind of feel like we have to now."

I'm not sure if it's the lingering effects of having a tree literally catch my fall, or if it's the puppy-dog eyes that she's throwing at me, but I can feel myself slowly starting to concede.

"Fine. I'll get a tree," I grumble.

"You will?" she asks, clearly delighted.

"Sure." I nod. Her satisfied expression makes the corner of my mouth lift up, and I don't bother to tamper it back down. I like that she's happy, despite still feeling unsure about this whole idea.

"And one of those reindeer statues for your front yard?"

"Absolutely not. Just the tree."

"Fair enough." Tori waves over a staff member to come help us cut and bale the tree.

A woman riding a small tractor not much farther down our lane responds with a wave and pulls to a stop next to us in no time.

"Hey! I'm Becky. Did you find your tree?" She hops down. She's wearing short denim overalls with the farm logo embroidered on the front pocket. A white T-shirt peeks out from underneath, and a red scarf ties her long blonde hair back in a ponytail. She looks cute and chipper, which, unfortunately for me, must be things that I'm attracted to because I can feel my throat starting to close up.

"The tree found us," Tori says simply, and Becky nods like that's a regular occurrence around here. I watch as she glances over at me and gives me a not-so-subtle once-over. When her gaze reaches mine, my cheeks heat up, and I give her a tight-lipped smile. Without a work scenario or a real estate conversation to fall back on, I can feel my confidence start to slip. It's not lost on me that, despite stumbling in front of Tori, I now feel ten times more uncomfortable in this moment under Becky's stare.

"Let me just grab my saw," she says, walking to the trailer connected to the tractor.

"She's cute," Tori whispers, coming to my side with a twinkle in her eye. "I saw her checking you out. You should totally practice flirting with her. Couldn't hurt, right?"

Before my adamant refusal can leave my mouth, Becky returns with a saw and starts assessing where to place it on the tree trunk.

"This tree is perfect for my brother's house," Tori says, lying to presumably let the woman know that I'm fair game.

"I'm glad you found what you're looking for," Becky says in a perky voice as she starts cutting into the trunk.

"Offer to help," Tori says in my ear. "Women love a strong man."

"I'd be happy to do that if you want," I offer, not necessarily because of Tori's suggestion but mostly because I feel like I should be doing something. I feel bad just standing by, watching her do all the work.

"Oh, I got it," Becky assures with a smile. "It's policy. Although, you definitely do look strong enough to easily cut down a tree."

The bold flirtation makes my mind go blank, and my chest tighten. After clearing my throat, I muster a lame, "Um, thanks."

"Smooth," Tori whispers, and I shoot her a glare. "So, how long have you been working here, Becky?"

"Pretty much my whole life. My grandpa started this farm, so I grew up on this land. It took years of begging, but eventually, they let me graduate from the concessions manager to part of the grounds crew. Been running it for a few years now."

"Good for you! We love a strong woman, don't we, Connor?" Tori nudges me with her elbow.

I nod, unable to think of the correct response to that question, but I can't help but show an amused smile. I somehow find Tori's meddling both irritating and oddly endearing all at once.

I keep my mouth shut as Tori and Becky continue chatting away. Becky manages to cut down and bale the tree all by herself, vehemently refusing help from either of us.

"Is this all you need?" Becky asks after hauling the tree into the trailer.

"Actually, we do need another tree," Tori says, turning toward me.

"The real reason we're here," I agree. "I'm not good at this kind of stuff. Do you have a vision of where it'll go at Makana Manor? What size do we need?"

Her eyes roam back and forth, deep in thought for a few seconds before she perks up. "The foyer," she says with certainty. "Guests will see it as soon as they walk in, and how gorgeous will it be with those vaulted ceilings?"

"Works for me," I agree with a nod, envisioning it in that spot perfectly.

"We'll need a pretty big one to fill the space," Tori says before turning to Becky. "Can you take us to the tallest tree you have?"

9

TORI

"The door should be unlocked," Connor says through a grunt, his arm muscles flexing around the tree as he shifts it in his arms to get a better grip. I rush ahead, right past the glistening pool in his backyard, and weave around the patio furniture to pull his back sliding door open.

"It's open. You sure you don't want help?" I ask, moving to the side as he shuffles closer to the door.

"I got it," he forces out.

"Is this some kind of alpha-male thing where you're trying to prove that you can carry an entire tree just because Becky can?"

"Nope."

"Because that's stupid, you know. I offered to help."

"I said I got it." He maneuvers himself and the tree inside. I follow, sliding the door shut behind me. After my eyes adjust to coming inside and out of the direct sunlight, my gaze immediately settles on the light-blue hue of his mostly bare walls. A lone couch—albeit a fancy-looking leather one—sits to the right, facing the wall where a plasma TV hangs. There's no coffee table, storage units, or even shelving, just a small glass end table next to the couch with nothing on it.

On the left is a simple gray-and-white kitchen with a small round kitchen table just off to the side. Everything is minimalistic and sparse, yet still somehow gives off an air of sophistication.

"Well, looks like we won't need to move any furniture around to fit the tree," I tease as I take it all in.

"What do you mean?" Connor sets the tree on the hardwood floor with a huff and looks at me with confusion.

"How do I say this delicately… There's not a whole lot in here."

His head swivels side to side, looking around before shrugging. "Like I said. It's only me—"

"Only you," I say in unison with a snort. "I know."

"Where do you want it?" he asks, and I bite back a smile at the fact that he's asking me.

"Hmm. This corner is perfect." I point to the wall next to the TV. "That way you can enjoy it while you're watching a television show, and you'll even be able to see a little bit of it when you're swimming in the pool."

His shrug of indifference confirms my suspicion that those are two things he doesn't do often anyway.

"Works for me."

I grab the stand and set it up, then help guide the tree stump in before clamping it into place. When I peer up from my crouched position on the floor, I catch a glimpse of Connor's profile as he's straightening a few branches and making sure that it's secure. Sunlight peering in through the window frames the outline of his face, illuminating his rugged features. He purses his lips together in pure concentration, deepening the tiny line that runs next to his mouth and making his eyes darken slightly with intensity.

It suddenly strikes me how truly good-looking he is and how it's absolutely insane that he doesn't take advantage of that in the dating department. It's not like women aren't interested. I've seen it with my own eyes. With a face that is definitely characterized as handsome by any standards, it's such a shame that he lacks the confidence to go with it. He has no reason for that whatsoever. It doesn't seem fair that I get to see the open, friendly side of him when it seems like not many other people do outside of work.

"I'm guessing you don't have any ornaments around here, do you?" I ask as I come to a stand, admiring the tree placement.

"Actually, I have three flat storage containers filled with ornaments under my bed right now."

"Seriously?"

"No, of course not."

I use the back of my hand to slap him teasingly on the arm. "No problem. We can get you some ornaments when we pick some up for the big tree."

"Or we can just leave it like this. I promise you, it's all the same to me."

"Well, that's pathetic and absolutely not happening. I won't be able to sleep at night if I know you're all alone over here, sharing a space with a sad, holiday-cheer-sucking tree."

"I'd manage just fine. Trust me."

I shrug, tucking a loose curl behind my ear as I casually look around, finding it thrilling that I get this rare glimpse into his personal life.

"Want to give me a tour of the rest of your house quickly before we leave? I'm dying to see more of what makes Connor, Connor."

"Sure." He shrugs, gesturing toward the hallway off the

kitchen. "There's not much to see, though. It won't be very interesting."

"You mean the rest of your house isn't as exciting as your vibrantly decorated living room? That's shocking," I say in mock outrage before smiling. "But really, I didn't peg you for being someone who doesn't know how to furnish a house. What kind of real estate expert are you anyway?"

"The kind that prefers a minimalistic style," he says without missing a beat.

"Touché." I nod absentmindedly, finding comfort in the easygoing banter that always flows between us. Spending this extra time together has only further enforced how much I enjoy being around him. If only I could find someone exactly like him outside of work that would be single and available. Then I might actually move dating off the back-burner.

"Down this hallway is a bathroom and a guest bedroom," he says, breezing past the open doorways before stopping briefly at the end of the hall and pivoting back in the other direction.

"My room," he says casually before walking back, pausing just long enough for me to peek my head in and catch a glimpse of a clean, organized space with, once again, minimal furniture, as well as a king-sized bed that's settled under the window. Scurrying to catch up to him, I follow him back through the kitchen.

"My office and a third bedroom are down that hallway, and then that door leads to the garage." He lifts his shoulders, turning his hands up. "I guess that's about it. Unless you want a closer look at the pool?"

"Sure." I follow him out the sliding doors into the blistering heat and bright sunshine. The rectangular pool that's right in the center of his backyard is glistening and majorly tempting, inadvertently pulling me toward it. Connor's phone rings just as he slides the door shut behind us.

"I've gotta take this, sorry," he mumbles, holding a finger up to excuse himself. I nod, wandering between two lounge chairs to the very edge of the pool.

"Frank, you know that's not going to work for my clients. They requested a thirty-day close, and now you expect them to close in seven days? That's insane."

I bring my hand above my eyes, shielding them from the sun, and watch as he pinches the bridge of his nose, pacing back and forth in front of a charcoal grill. His eyes convey the same intensity they had earlier when he was focusing on the tree, and I smile at how easily he can shift into savage work mode. The contrast between how he is when he's attempting to flirt versus how he is when he's in business mode is amazing. Imagine if he could channel this intensity and confidence toward his dating life. The thought alone causes a rogue shiver to run down my spine.

I brush it off and lower to sit, slipping my feet into the water, relishing the cool rush it sends up my legs.

"I'm telling you, that's unacceptable, Frank. Talk to your clients and call me back as soon as possible."

I can practically hear the scowl on his face without even turning my head. After a moment, he drops next to me, sliding his shoes off and slipping his legs under the water too.

"Everything alright?" I ask, plastering a smile on my face.

"Fine." He shakes his head, dismissing his frustration.

"I like your place," I say, happy to change the subject.

"Even without the appropriate amount of furniture?" He smirks, the tension starting to fade from his body.

"Even so. And it's even better now that it has a Christmas tree." I nudge his arm with my elbow, which elicits another smile.

"Speaking of which, we should probably get the big tree over to Makana Manor, huh?" he asks.

"Good idea." I glance at my Apple Watch and notice the

time. "It's getting kind of late. What do you think about unloading it and then going back tomorrow to decorate?"

"Sounds like a plan," he agrees with a nod. "My morning is booked up with an open house from ten to noon, though."

"I have a meeting with a potential seller around one. Should we meet later in the afternoon?"

"Works for me." He comes to a stand and offers his hand, just like he did when we were in the bathtub, and helps me to stand. "Let's go unload this thing."

10

TORI

"You got the stack of gala invites that I set on your desk last night, right?" Connor asks as he's bent over the pile of plastic bags that are filled with brightly colored ornaments, tropical flowers, and other tree decor with varying traditional Hawaiian style. The bags are overflowing and spread out widely on the shiny marble floor. He pulls off a tag from a large glittery green ball ornament and hands it to me.

"Yes. Thank you for printing those. I addressed and sent them out this morning—all three hundred of them," I say, taking the ornament from him and finding the perfect branch to hang it on.

"Perfect. And I created a spreadsheet to start marking RSVPs as they come in, so just let me know when you get one, and we'll make note of it." His deep voice causes a slight echo as it bounces off the high-vaulted ceilings in the entryway of Makana Manor.

"Oh, look at that one." I grab a glittery flip-flop ornament the size of my foot from his outstretched hand.

"That is very sparkly," he says in a monotone with a blank expression, and I have to stifle a giggle.

"This is probably the very last activity you want to be doing, isn't it?" I ask.

"I would rather be doing literally anything else," he agrees. "But I'll suck it up for the sake of this listing and the open house. This'll be the best-decorated tree Oahu's ever seen."

"That's the spirit. Hey, did you see they started setting up for the Kapolei City Lights parade? I think it starts tomorrow night." My mind starts running through the many different seasonal activities around town that are starting this week, even though I really have no intention of going to any of them. As amazing as Oahu is this time of year, I have a feeling this gala will be occupying most of my time this year.

The song "Mele Kalikimaka" is playing softly around us from the house-wide sound system, creating a festive ambiance while we chat and decorate.

"Didn't really notice, honestly. I haven't been to that in years," he admits.

"It's been a while for me too." I grab a pinkish-white poinsettia and tuck it between branches next to some greenery I had already added to the tree. "I used to go all the time when I was a kid, though."

Another Christmas song passes as we work in a comfortable, quiet rhythm to bring a beautifully decorated tree to life one kitschy ornament at a time.

"Oh shoot," I say, a thought suddenly occurring to me. "I can't believe we forgot to get ornaments for your tree, too, while we were at the store."

Connor looks entirely unfazed, ripping the tag off the next ornament. "I was hoping you weren't going to remember."

"I'll have to make a separate trip," I say.

"Please don't," he says with a laugh. "I'll order some on my own."

"Why do I feel like you're just saying that?"

"I'll do my best. Please don't worry about it. Now take this huge ornament." He hands me a large ukulele ornament, and I scan the tree for an open branch.

"So, tell me a little more about you, Connor. Seeing your house makes me want to know more about the non-work side of your life. I'm sure it's as fascinating as your decorating style."

"What do you want to know?" He shrugs, ignoring my teasing jab while handing me a glass surfboard ornament.

"What do you like to do for fun?"

"Does closing deals count?" He rifles through the bag in front of him, sticking his hand all the way to the bottom.

"Nope."

With a deep sigh, he stands and comes to my side, bringing a handful of ornaments with him before cringing. "Is it sad that I can't think of anything?"

"Yes, it is," I answer without pause.

"When I think of fun, I think of work, truthfully. The high I get when finally closing a tough negotiation. The prospect of a new property listing. It's such a rush, don't you think?"

"I mean, obviously, I agree with you there. I get it. I really do. But you're telling me there's nothing outside of work that brings you joy?"

"I should probably be more embarrassed at the fact that I'm constantly glued to my phone than I really am. Work has taken over the majority of my life for a while now. But truthfully, it's hard to find any regrets. My work ethic has gotten me pretty far."

"Okay, so hypothetically, if you had free time, for some crazy reason, what would you do?"

"Hmm. I guess I'd find more time to watch a sports game here and there," he offers.

"There ya go. Did you play any sports growing up?"

"Baseball. I haven't played since I was thirteen, but I loved it." His words come out with a hint of nostalgia.

"Why'd you stop playing?"

"I started working," he says with a shrug. "My dad's business partner offered me fifty bucks one day to sweep, dust, and empty the garbage in his office when a big client was just about to show up unannounced. I stopped by every day after that, and for whatever reason, he had a new job for me to do each day. It got to the point where either he or my dad would teach me a valuable lesson about business while I did the tasks. From then on, I was hooked. Work trumped everything else."

"Aw, that makes me a little sad for younger you. What about having fun or just being a kid?"

He shrugs. "Just wasn't a priority for me, I guess. What about you? What do you do for fun?"

"If I'm not working, I'm typically either with my family or off with friends."

"Right on." He hands me an ornament of Santa in a Hawaiian shirt and flip-flops. I slide it onto a branch just as my phone buzzes from inside my purse that's lying on the floor. I wipe my glittery hands on my shorts as I go to answer it.

"Tori, it's Charlene," the voice of a fellow agent from Maui chirps in my ear when I answer. "I just saw your invitation to the holiday-themed gala, and I wanted to personally send in my RSVP for yes. What a wonderful idea. And that estate! My goodness, I can't wait to see it in person."

"That's great, Charlene!"

"I have a buyer in mind, so go ahead and put me down for two guests."

"Awesome. Thanks for letting me know. I can't wait to see you there!"

After disconnecting, I slide my phone back into my purse. "Well, I'd say we're off to a good start. We've got two confirmed guests already for the gala."

"Awesome. All it takes is that one perfect buyer, right?"

"That's right. Real Estate 101," I say, placing the last green sparkly ornament on the tree.

"I'll mark her RSVP on the spreadsheet when I get back to the office tonight." Connor offers as he fluffs a branch.

"Thanks." I start collecting garbage and empty bags from the floor. "We'll have to sweep up this glitter before we head out. Beth's bringing a client through for a showing tonight."

"That's right. I'll grab the broom. I think I remember seeing one in here." He finds the small entryway closet and opens it to pull out the broom and dustpan.

"So, I'm glad we got the tree up and decorated, but what do you say we wait to decorate the rest of the house until right before the gala? I'd hate to have the other agents benefit off our hard work, you know?" I ask.

"I'm with you on that. They know we're planning the event, obviously, but it would be stupid to decorate it early just for them to bring their own clients through beforehand," he agrees.

"Exactly." I stand back to admire the tree as Connor finishes sweeping. "So, tomorrow, I'll confirm the menu with the catering company."

"Okay, and I'll call the rental place and increase the number of how many high-tops we need. We definitely need a few out by the pool," he says.

"Great. We make a good team, don't we?" I ask proudly, placing my hands on my hips.

"We do," he says with a smile, his warm green eyes connecting with mine.

I return the smile as I further confirm that thought in my mind. I usually like to work solo, especially when it comes to planning open houses, but this has been a really nice experience so far with him. Obviously, it doesn't hurt that he's so easy to look at, either. I caught myself staring at the profile of his face again for just a second too long when he was putting the star on top of the tree earlier. The focus and intensity of his eyes was just so darn distracting. I must usually have work blinders on, but since we've been spending so much more time together lately, those blinders aren't quite so thick anymore, despite my best efforts to keep my thoughts as professional as I can.

"I say we call it a day, huh?" he asks, pulling me out of my wandering mind and standing back to admire the tree.

"Let's. I'll call you in the morning to check in." It's not lost on me that I'm already looking forward to that next conversation. I'm getting used to having Connor around. So much so that when I get home later that evening and start to unwind—complete with a glass of wine on the balcony and a fresh pile of mysterious Christmas cards—it all feels just a tad bit too quiet.

11

CONNOR

"Yes, the views are incredible on this property. There are floor-to-ceiling windows in almost every room, and you get coastal views with just about every one of them," I say into the phone to Jay, a realtor from Texas who reached out after seeing the Makana Manor listing on one of the social media blasts that Tori and I sent out this morning.

"It sure sounds like a fantastic piece of real estate. I'm guessing the price is what's keeping it on the market, right?" Jay asks. "Any chance the owner is willing to come down at all?"

"I mean, it wouldn't hurt to try. You know how things work. If you send me your best offer, I legally have to present it to my client, so you're more than welcome to do that, but I'll tell you right now, he's not very keen on budging from where he's at price-wise."

"That's what I thought," Jay murmurs to himself.

"But honestly, this house is worth every single penny of that dollar amount," I say, trying to salvage what's left of this potential deal. "You won't find a more luxurious property in all of Hawaii, that's for sure."

"Yeah." He lets out a disgruntled huff, and the last sliver of optimism slowly slips away. "Well, I'll keep it in mind and let you know if my clients are interested."

"Sounds good. Thanks, Jay. Take care." I toss my phone onto my desk and extend my arms over my head, clasping my hands around the back of my neck, stretching in an attempt to relieve the tension that built up over that call. When I swivel my chair toward Tori, I find her watching me with her elbow resting on the arm of her chair, her hand holding her head up by the chin. Her mouth is pulled into a sympathetic half-smile.

"Any luck?" she asks, raising her eyebrows.

"Not really. He was stuck on the price, just like the last several phone calls we've gotten." It's hard to not feel a little bit discouraged with each disappointing phone call that we get.

"That's alright," she says, clapping her hands together once, perking up, and turning back toward her laptop. "He's not our buyer." I can't help but smile at her enthusiasm.

"Auntie Tori!" A young boy comes flying down the aisle toward us, screeching to a halt as he runs into the side of Tori's chair. A man and woman trail behind, the man holding a little girl in his arms.

"Elliot!" Tori exclaims, her eyes lighting up with surprise and her arms wrapping around him. I've never seen her with a smile as bright and wide as the one that's beaming on her face at this very moment. She seems absolutely lit up from the inside out, accentuating how beautiful she really is. I get momentarily distracted by the look on her face and the way looking at her makes me feel—even though I can't exactly place what this feeling is. My professionalism kicks back in, and I clear my throat, turning back toward my laptop to give them some privacy.

"What are you doing here?" I hear her ask.

"We're on our way to the Kapolei City Lights parade," Elliot says. "I wanted to ask you to come with us, but Dad said the odds of you saying yes were better if we came in person. Otherwise, you probably wouldn't pull yourself away from work."

"Did he now?" Tori addresses the man, who I'm guessing is her brother, Matt, based on what she's told me about Elliot.

"Yup," Matt replies confidently. "Want to come? I guess the whole family is going."

"Oh, I'm not sure, guys," she says regretfully. "I've got about thirty emails left to go through before leaving tonight, and Connor and I have some things to discuss. This is Connor, by the way."

At the mention of my name, I turn and offer a smile and quick wave to her family. "Hi, how's it going?"

"Hey, why don't you come too?" Elliot asks after not so casually giving me a once-over. I wasn't exactly expecting the invitation, so I falter, trying to think of the best way to let him down easily.

"It'll be fun! I promise," he says eagerly, looking back and forth between Tori and me. An incoming email pings on my Apple Watch, and when I flick my gaze down, it tells me that it's five-fifteen. I usually don't stop working for another three hours at least, and that would be on a good night. With a laugh, Tori glances over at me, and I smile back in return.

"I'm sure Connor has other things to do this evening, Elliot," she says, breaking eye contact with me and ruffling his hair.

"Please? The parade starts at six. We have to go soon so we don't miss it!"

When Tori's eyes flick up to meet mine again, I realize that a tiny part of me is excited at the prospect of hanging out with her more this evening. An evening with a friend away from work would probably be good for me, anyway. At least I know my parents would be proud if I did. I fight the years of conditioning that are telling me to stay at work and blurt out, "I'll go if you go."

"Really?" she asks in surprise, a twinkling gleam of excitement surfacing underneath the disbelief.

"Why not?" I nod, feeling more certain by the second. "I trust my new friend, Elliot, and if he says that it'll be that great, then I'm pretty sure we don't want to miss it. You walked to work today, right?

"Yeah," she says, still wary.

"Come on. I can drive us. We can go over some gala stuff on the way."

~

"Look at you. Connor Brooks. At a non-work event, seemingly enjoying himself. Never thought I'd see the day." Tori nudges me with her elbow as we walk along the people-filled sidewalk that's lined with food trucks and various local vendors. The block party that precedes the parade is overflowing with locals and tourists alike while loud music fills the streets.

I push my sunglasses on top of my head, the glaring sun becoming less aggressive as it slowly starts its descent for the evening. I'm thankful that I wore khaki shorts today to work instead of pants, as the polo shirt I'm wearing has kept me hot enough.

"Hey, I know how to have fun—at least, I think I remember how to," I chuckle.

"How does it feel to let loose a little and not be doing something for work?"

"To be fair, I've mentally envisioned closing three deals and came up with a solid marketing plan for my listing on Apine Street just in the walk here from the car," I admit.

"Seriously?" Tori drops her jaw open in surprise. "What

about the whole time I was talking to you? Were you tuning me out?"

"You mean when you were telling me about the very specific way you enjoy your smoothie bowls? Riveting stuff, but I did, in fact, tune you out by the time you mentioned the fourth strawberry slice."

"Well, that's rude," she huffs.

"Sorry." I smile. "Having been your cubicle-mate for this long, tuning out your rambling stories is a skill that I've acquired."

"Hey, I have a challenge." She perks up with a surge of newfound energy. "How about this whole evening you try to forget about work? Let the phone calls go to voicemail. Leave the emails unread. And I'll do the same. It'll be fun!"

"That sounds excruciatingly painful." I'm hoping my flat tone accurately conveys how I feel about that idea.

"Worth a try, though, don't you think? The emails can wait! Let's try and be well-rounded individuals with balanced lives for once, huh?"

"What for?"

"To prove we can do it. Maybe we'll discover that it's not all it's cracked up to be, and then you can go back to your sad little loveless, work-obsessed life."

"Hey!" I clutch at my chest, feigning insult.

"Sorry, that was harsh." Her genuine regretful smile makes me laugh. I get caught on the way her nose crinkles as she looks at me, and for whatever reason, I follow the sudden urge I have to concede and make her happy.

"Alright. You're on," I give in, hoping that I'm not being too optimistic in assuming that I can handle an hour or two of no work. "No phone calls, emails, or talk about the listing."

"Yay." She claps her hands together in excitement as I slow to let her walk in front of me, letting a group of people squeeze by in the opposite direction. We walk single-file through a large crowd that's huddled in front of the shrimp taco truck and then round the street corner to where chairs are lined up along the sidewalk, ready for the parade.

"Alright." Tori turns back to me. "Are you ready to meet my family?"

12

TORI

"Sorry, that was just me." I bare a cheesy, hesitant smile, peering over nervously to gauge Connor's reaction. He's visibly agitated and uncomfortable, trying to ignore the ringing phone in his pocket. "I was just testing you."

"Are you kidding me?" he says in a hushed, exasperated tone, clearly not amused by my antics yet not wanting to make a scene. He runs his hands along the sides of his shorts as if his hands need to keep busy and distracted if he's not to reach for his phone. "Are you trying to torture me?"

"Not on purpose." I crinkle my nose as I shrug my shoulders apologetically, ignoring his eye roll as I cancel the outgoing phone call to him. I scoop a spoonful of shave ice into my mouth and notice Grace eyeing us from where she's sitting on the other side of Connor on the curb where we're waiting for the parade to start. The rest of my family is lined up in a row next to her.

Everyone is squished together, along with the rest of the island, it seems, on the jam-packed curb.

"So, Connor…" Grace starts, and a subtle hint of uneasiness hits me with a jolt, leaving me apprehensive about what she's about to say. "Did you know that Tori was voted 'best catch' in high school?"

"Grace," I grumble an irritated warning, already knowing and dreading where she's going with this.

"As in, any guy would be lucky to have her," she continues matter-of-factly.

"Is that so?" Connor's interest piques as he engages with Grace, much to my dismay.

"Yup. I tend to agree with that assessment too. She's smoking hot, don't you think?"

"Grace," I try one more time to put a stop to her prying.

"I'd say that's a fair assumption," Connor says. "Although, it's recently come to my attention that she has a bad habit of meddling." He sets his empty shave ice bowl on the ground by his feet. "I am now the owner of a real-life Christmas tree in my living room that I had no intention of caring for. So I'd say that takes a few points away."

"That sounds about right." Grace laughs.

"What sounds right?" Emily cranes her neck to join the conversation.

"Connor and I were just talking about what a catch Tori is."

"Oh, she totally is." Emily smiles, her brows dancing. "Although, one might view her dairy allergy as a sign of weakness."

"Okay, okay." I stand abruptly, pulling Connor's arm on my way up, ready to put some distance between us and my sisters. "Let's go grab something to drink." Connor just laughs as he follows me with an amused expression on his face.

"Remember when I mentioned that my family doesn't

respect boundaries?" I roll my eyes as we squeeze through a group of people standing on the sidewalk.

"I kind of wanted to hear what they were going to say next, though," Connor quips, falling into place next to me. Darkness has officially covered the night, with green and red twinkling lights strung around a few food trucks and vendor tables, as well as up the base of several palm trees. Live music is booming from speakers, filling the air with traditional Hawaiian Christmas music as we walk along.

"I assure you it would not have been useful information."

"Maybe not to you," he says. "So, Emily is the one getting married soon, right?"

"Yes, in the spring," I confirm.

He nods in return. "Just trying to keep track of everyone."

We come to a stop in front of a festive lit-up sign near a vendor truck. "You want a Rudolph Spritzer?" Connor asks.

"Sure." I stand with him in line, quietly enjoying the live music that feels like it's beating in my chest. The scent of fried food and sugary treats hangs heavy in the air. We get to the front of the line, where he orders and pays, then hands me the vodka drink with orange juice, cranberry, cherry juice, and ginger ale all mixed together, creating one of my favorite refreshing holiday drinks. We continue walking on, wandering aimlessly between people as the first lit-up vehicles in the parade start making their way down the street.

"So I saw Rich in the break room today," I say.

"Oh yeah? How did that go?" he asks, taking a sip of his drink.

"He was adding to the communal Makana Manor calendar on the wall in the break room. He's planning to host an open house a few days before our gala."

"You're kidding."

"I know, rude, right? That only gives us a couple days to set up." I take a sip of my spritzer, the fizzy bubbles tickling the inside of my nose. "Oh, shoot. We're not supposed to be talking about work."

"Good. Does that mean I won? Is the challenge over now? Can I check my phone?" He lifts his hand in the air, and I instinctively loop my arm around his, holding it in place so he won't reach for his phone.

"Absolutely not." I laugh. "This is good for you. For us. A little work detox." His bicep muscles flex underneath my arm, and a small zing of electricity hits my stomach at the movement. As comfortable and natural as it feels to be touching him in this way, I'm also conscious of not crossing a line, so I slowly release my grip and bring both hands back around my drink, attempting to ignore the lingering flutter in my stomach.

The crowds start to thin, and the music becomes quieter as we near the end of the street, where the parade route comes to an end. I can't quite put my finger on it, but something feels different with Connor tonight. Maybe it's because of the darkness of the night, or maybe it's because there's no involvement of work and our professional life, but it feels more intimate somehow. More personal. Like we could maybe be something more if our circumstances were different.

"Do you want to head back to your family?" Connor asks. Shaking my head, I drop to sit on an open stretch of the curb.

"I don't think so." I look up at him, finding his eyes in the darkness, and smile. "I kinda like the quiet over here." After meeting and holding my stare for an extra second, he nods and lowers himself to sit next to me. He stretches out his legs onto the street, and his arm presses lightly against mine, despite there being plenty of room on the curb for him to spread out.

We watch as a set of fire trucks with flashing lights comes down the street and passes by, and I fight the urge to press even closer to him. I feel this tugging of a spark with him that I've never noticed before, and it seems to be lurking and tempting me at every turn tonight. But work comes first, and I refuse to do anything unprofessional or anything that might risk our work relationship. And even though I know he feels the same about dating in the workplace, he also doesn't move away or put space between us, seemingly content to be pressed against my side.

I like this closeness that I feel to him here tonight, outside of work—no rules or expectations or lines that shouldn't be crossed. Like tonight, we're allowed to just be Connor and Tori. Friends. Coworkers. Or maybe the potential for something more, even though I know it's not a real possibility.

A car that's almost completely covered with stuck-on wreaths comes next in the line of the parade, with people walking alongside it and throwing candy to kids. I see my nieces and nephew up the road, scrambling to pick up the candy off the street.

With a smile, I relax even more next to Connor, watching and admiring each vehicle as it passes by, feeling the warmth of his body lightly pressing into mine. I'm not sure what this new energy between us means, but I'm content to just sit in it while I can. Even after the parade is over and the mayor has lit the fifty-foot Christmas tree at the tree-lighting ceremony, we stay next to each other on the curb, sipping on our Rudolph Spritzers and enjoying this solitary moment well into the night.

13

CONNOR

"I'm really starting to think twice about doing any kind of shopping with you," I say to Tori as we walk to my parked Tesla, several overflowing bags stuffed under our arms.

"Why?" she asks innocently, clearly not seeing a problem with the animalistic way she just threw copious amounts of wreath-making material into the cart at record speed. A variety of flowers and foliage hangs out of the bags, along with scissors, a special kind of glue, and other supplies that are completely foreign to me.

"Hey, if we're going to make some traditional Hawaiian Christmas wreaths for our gala guests to take home, then I am committing myself one thousand percent to making sure they are the most amazing wreaths in the entire world." She gives me a pointed look. "You should totally be matching my energy on this."

"I think my excitement level over DIY-ing wreaths is as high as it can possibly go." I stuff the bags into the car before climbing in and starting it. I turn the air conditioning up as Tori adjusts one of the vents in her direction. A waft of vanilla fills the car as the air blows through her hair, and I try to ignore the way I'm all of a sudden tempted to take a deep breath in.

She gets buckled and smooths out the cream-colored linen pants she's wearing that she paired with a tight white bodysuit tank. She looks incredibly put-together, and I wonder how hard it is to put a professional wardrobe together while also trying to stay cool in this heat. I'm sure it's much harder for her than it is for me with my standard wardrobe of khaki shorts and button-up shirts. I'm definitely not envious of her in that aspect.

"It's going to be great," she says with a smile, sliding her sunglasses on.

"So you keep telling me."

"Oh, before we go, I have to show you this picture that Paige sent me. They brought the kids to see Santa arrive by canoe over in Waikiki, and she got the cutest picture of Elliot and Noelle with Santa," she says, pulling out her phone. She holds it up to me, and I smile at a picture of the kids next to Santa, who's wearing flip-flops, shorts, and sunglasses.

"That's cute," I say, shifting into reverse. "I remember doing that as a kid."

I'm just pulling out of the parking lot on our way back to the office when my phone rings. I accept the call on the hands-free Bluetooth option, and my grandma's voice fills the car.

"Connor?" she asks, and I can immediately tell she's flustered.

"Yeah, Grandma? I'm right here. What's going on?"

"Oh, I'm so sorry to bother you. I dropped my pill bottle on the floor, and now I've got a whole mess of pills everywhere and a bunch rolled under the refrigerator. How do I get those out? Should I try to stick my cane under there and scoop them out?"

"No, don't do that—" I warn.

"Betty, we have people we can call for assistance. Quit bothering the poor boy," Grandpa's voice can be heard in the background.

"I'm just going to try my cane…" Grandma's voice wanders off.

"Betty, do not bend over," Grandpa speaks before I can. "Remember what happened last time you tried to pick something up? We couldn't get you off the floor for hours."

"Grandma," I try to get her attention but, once again, can't get a word in.

"Oh, stop, Louie. I'll be just fine."

The light tap of Tori's hand on my forearm brings me out of my thoughts, and I swerve my attention over to her.

"Do you want to go?" she whispers, pointing at the speakers. I hesitate, trying to assess the situation.

"You wouldn't mind?" I ask her quietly, just loud enough to be heard over my grandparents' bickering. "It's just right up the street." I feel bad about making Tori come with me, but my grandma is stubborn enough to prove that she's still capable of doing anything, and more often than not, that doesn't end well.

"Not at all," Tori whispers, waving her hands in assurance.

"Okay, Grandma, I'm on my way," I say to no one in particular, as it seems the phone has been cast to the side. Their arguing voices are muffled and seem farther away. After hanging up, I throw a regretful smile Tori's way.

"Sorry about this."

"Gosh, don't worry about it. I don't mind. Besides, I've gotta see how this plays out. There's nothing worse than pills under the fridge."

My phone rings again, and instead of my grandma, this time it's a client of mine whose house we just put on the market last week. Answering the phone is like an automatic impulse for me, so I answer and try to make the phone call as quick as possible, not wanting to be rude with Tori in the car. I wrap up the phone call in record time.

When we arrive at the assisted living building, we walk through the front doors, and the look on Ruth's face makes me instantly regret not asking Tori to wait in the car.

"Connor, who's your fr—" she starts.

"Sorry, Ruth, can't stop today," I say with a polite wave.

Tori gives her a friendly wave as she follows me into the elevator and up to my grandparents' floor. We rush down the hall, and I waste no time pushing their door open.

"Grandma?" I call out, rounding the corner to see my grandpa on his hands and knees, with Grandma crouching over to direct him.

"There's one right there. Do you see it, Louie?" She's pointing to a small spot on the floor.

"No, Betty, I do not see it. The pills are the same color as the damn floor. You couldn't have dropped the bright-orange ones?" Grandpa grumbles.

"What in the world are you doing on the floor?" I ask, skirting around Grandma to help him up. "I thought you were the sane one?"

"Oh! Connor." Grandma straightens in surprise. "I wasn't expecting you."

"Yeah, well, someone's gotta keep an eye on you two."

I lift with a grunt, hooking my arm under his to get him all the way up. Grandma moves to the side, and then I watch as her eyes widen when her gaze lands on where Tori is standing off to the side.

"Oh. My. Heavens," she breathes, placing a hand on her chest. "I never thought I'd see the day. Louie, look. He brought a girl."

"She's not—" I start but barely get two words out.

"Will you look at this," she interrupts. "You are absolutely stunning. What's your name, dear?"

"I'm Tori," Tori says with a bright smile and a wave, stepping closer, clearly not bothered by the attention.

"Tori. My word. You are just the spitting image of Grace Kelly. Don't you think so, Louie?" she asks, clearly not expecting an actual response as she continues on. "Connor, you didn't tell me you have a lady friend—"

"I don't." My words hang uselessly in the air as she interrupts again.

"This is so exciting. Come, please sit." Grandma shuffles to the kitchen table, gesturing toward a chair for Tori. I guide Grandpa to a chair, and then I sink reluctantly into the one between him and Tori, bracing myself for the conversation to come.

"Grandma, Tori and I aren't dating. We're co-workers," I explain, making eye contact with her to ensure that she's listening. Saying the words 'Tori' and 'dating' out loud in the same sentence causes an uneasiness in my gut. Not because the idea is off-putting but more so because it isn't. And I haven't been able to wrap my head around that fact for the last couple of days, especially since the parade, where I very clearly gravitated toward being as close to her as possible. Something about her that night kept pulling me in, an invisible force that pushed against my natural instinct to shy away from her, and my brain has been a little cloudy when I think about it ever since.

"Uh-huh. That's nice, dear." Her doe-eyed, blank expression has me questioning whether my words are even registering behind her sweet smile.

"We're working on that big listing together. Remember the one I told you about?"

"Uh-huh." She nods before turning to Tori. "So tell me about yourself. Did you grow up on the island?"

"Alright," I mumble to myself, tapping the table as I stand. I feel the sudden urge to move things along so we can get out of here as soon as possible.

"I did—for most of my life anyway. We moved here when I was a kid," Tori replies cheerfully.

I crouch down and pick up the pills, scooping them into my open palm one at a time while they chat away easily behind me. I half listen to them cover the topics of Tori's childhood, the weather, and upcoming Christmas traditions.

"So, tell me, what drew you to my Connor?" Grandma rests her chin in her palm, gazing at Tori like she's the most interesting thing she's ever seen. "What do you like about him?"

"Okay," I interrupt, picking up the last pill at the perfect time. "Time to go."

"Already?" Tori asks, unfazed and—dare I say—enjoying my grandparents' wrongful assumptions. "Are you sure you got them all?"

"Yup. Let's head out." I walk briskly to her chair, pulling it out gently so that she's forced to stand.

"Oh. Well, it was lovely to meet you, sweetie," Grandma says. "Take care of that boy. Maybe you can convince Connor to stop by more often. It would be wonderful to see you again. Right, Louie?"

"Oh, yes," Grandpa chimes in just as I touch the handle of the front door, ushering Tori out in front of me.

"So nice to meet you both. Betty, please send me that recipe for that cranberry cobbler. It sounds delicious," Tori says with a wave.

"Okay, love you both. Bye," I say quickly, pressing my hand against Tori's back to move her along before shutting the door and exhaling a sharp breath.

"They are the absolute cutest," Tori gushes, falling into step next to me.

"They're something," I agree. "They kind of have a mind of their own most of the time."

"Ah, they're sweet."

When the elevator doors open back down on the main level, I

shouldn't be as surprised as I am to see that the couch that Ruth sits on is occupied by three additional people as well as four more on the opposite couch, all staring expectantly at Tori and me and whispering in hushed voices.

With a sigh, I guide Tori past their stares and out the front doors. I wonder if Grandma somehow sent out a building-wide silent signal about my 'new lady friend' or if Ruth lured them all on her own.

14

TORI

"I have a crush on Connor," I whine, falling face-first onto the bed in my parents' guest bedroom, blurting out the truth that I've been trying so hard to ignore the past few days.

"Well, duh," Grace says matter-of-factly from her criss-cross position on the floor, not even bothering to look up from the stack of photographs in her hand. We're utilizing this Sunday afternoon lunch to sort and collect photographs to display at Emily's wedding, even though she's not getting married until the spring. When she gets an idea in her head, she often gets adamant about completing it as soon as possible, and apparently, this particular task cannot possibly wait. Old picture boxes and photo albums are scattered across the floor as well as across the bed, where I pull myself up to sit.

"Ooh. So what does this mean? Are we making a move?" Ava asks excitedly.

"No." The firmness in my reply serves more as a reminder to

myself than anything toward her. "No way. No work relationships."

"But why, though?" she asks.

"For so many reasons. They always get complicated, and I don't see how they wouldn't interfere with productivity. Plus, what if we didn't work out? What if it got messy? I don't want to jeopardize my career and the status I've worked so hard to earn just to date somebody." Although, if I'm honest, despite my reasonings, I've been having a hard time forgetting the way I felt when Connor was pressed to my side at the parade and the way the butterflies seemed to grow wilder as the night went on and every day since.

"But don't you want a relationship eventually? Surely you don't want to be alone forever?" Paige asks from her spot on the floor by the dresser.

"Of course I do, but not at the risk of my career. And I know for a fact he would agree with me." I place a pillow on my lap and slide another stack of pictures in front of myself. "So I'll just have to get over it."

"Get over your crush…" Paige confirms slowly.

"Yes. Which majorly sucks. Have you met the guy? Why does he have to be all attractive and funny and…nice? Doesn't he know I'm trying to advance my career?" I push my fingertips into my hair, massaging my temples in an attempt to ease some tension.

"How rude of him to be so appealing," Emily chimes in.

"So rude." I shift my attention down and flip through photographs, stumbling upon several from our grandparents' wedding day that we've been searching for. "Bingo. I found them!"

One is an image of them standing side by side on the top step of a church. Grandma's bouquet of flowers is front and center, and Grandpa's hand is curled around her waist, a look of complete joy showing on both their faces. It will be perfect for

Emily's generational wedding day photo display that she plans to have at her wedding.

"Look at this one." I pass the picture to Grace, who then passes it on to Emily.

"Oh, that's perfect!" Emily says, placing it in the keep pile next to her. We already have wedding photos from our parents, so now we just need to find the pictures from our other grandparents' wedding day next. Before digging into another pile, I figure now is a good time for a quick break. A break from both photo searching and my wandering thoughts of Connor.

"I'm going to grab a drink. Anybody want anything?" I climb off the bed and head toward the door.

"I'll come with you," Paige says, trailing behind me as we head down the hallway. We come into the kitchen just as my mom, who's hunched over the kitchen counter toward Elliot, slaps her hand down on top of a large card pile.

"Slapjack!" she shouts before laughing.

"Oh, man!" Elliot cries. "How are you so good at this game?"

"She has many years of slapjack under her belt," I say, grabbing a water bottle from the fridge.

"It's the only game I've played more of than Go Fish," she confirms, straightening to stand as Elliot compiles the cards back into a stack.

"How is the picture gathering going in there?" Mom asks, sliding the charcuterie snack board she made in our direction.

"Great, we've found a few keepers," Paige says.

I grab an olive off the board and then move next to Elliot, sliding into the corner chair by the wall.

"Oh, Tori, did you get a Christmas card from the Samuels?" Mom asks, reaching to rifle through the pile of mail next to me.

"No, I haven't," I say as she hands me the card from our old neighbors. Their card shows several images of the family of four frolicking on the beach.

"Cute." I set it back down and reach for a cracker. "Hey, have you guys gotten any random cards this year? From people you don't know?"

"No." Paige shrugs.

"No, why do you ask?" Mom asks.

"There must be something screwed up at the post office. I've gotten so many random cards this year. Just yesterday, I got one from a family in Ypsilanti, Michigan, and one from a couple in Boulder, Colorado. Never seen these people before in my life, and they're all personally addressed to me."

"Well, that's odd," Mom says, furrowing her brows.

"Oh, that was me," Elliot says nonchalantly, grabbing for a stray playing card that fell out of the pile when he was shuffling. Shock hits me, and I twist my head in his direction.

"What do you mean, Elliot?" Paige inquires before I can.

"Yeah, that's because of me," he answers simply.

"Okay, I'm going to need you to explain that a little bit further, buddy." I turn so I'm facing where he sits next to me.

With a shrug, he continues. "There was a service project on the school bulletin board where you could nominate people who might be lonely this holiday season, and they would enter their info into a nation-wide database. Then, people from all over can access that database and send cards to whoever they want."

I blink at him, digesting what he just said. "And you think I'm lonely?"

"Maybe?"

"And why would that be?" I ask, trying to wrap my brain around why he would have done something like this.

"I dunno." He shrugs. "Because you're the only one not married or in a relationship. Grandma talks about it all the time. I didn't want you to feel alone at all—especially this time of year."

I'm torn between feeling embarrassed and extremely touched that he would go to such lengths just for me.

"Elliot, that is so sweet." I ruffle his hair, dipping my head to make eye contact. "But you didn't have to do that, buddy. I'm not lonely at all. I've got all of you to keep me company."

"Okay." Once again, he shrugs, completely unaffected. "I'm gonna go find Dad." He hops down and skips out of the room.

"That is really cute," Mom says, wiping at the corners of her eyes. "He is so thoughtful."

"He is," I agree. "Totally unnecessary, but still a sweet gesture."

"He's not wrong, you know. If you took some focus off of work, maybe you would find a nice young man to settle down with, and the rest of us wouldn't be left to wonder if you're lonely or not," Mom says pointedly.

With an exaggerated, slow eye roll, I try my best to smile. "We really don't need to get into this again, Mom. I'm perfectly happy with the way my life is right now, thank you very much." As much as I truly do believe that, Elliot's words echo in my mind. I can't help but think that maybe it might be time to start seriously dating. Not Connor, of course. Someone outside of work. But my family isn't wrong. If I want to find my person someday, it wouldn't hurt to put more of an effort into it and start looking.

"I'm excited for your open house gala," Paige offers, rescuing me by changing the subject, and I shoot her a grateful smile.

"I'm so happy you all can come. It's going to be beautiful."

"Any leads on the house yet?"

"We've had several people interested—a lot, actually. We've had a few private showings, but everyone shuts down when we tell them that the owner isn't willing to budge on price."

"Shoot. That's a tough position to be in," Paige says sympathetically.

"We have had a lot of interest on our social media channels, though, so that's a great sign. We've been doing lots of social media blasts, and we just sent out a newsletter on Friday, so there's been a lot of activity lately."

"Hey, you two are slacking on the job!" Ava yells from down the hallway. "These pictures aren't going to find themselves."

"We better head back in before they get mad." Paige laughs, and I slide out of my chair. I follow her out of the kitchen and down the hall to finish our sisterly bridesmaid duties for the afternoon, and all the while, I'm left with the nagging question in the back of my mind if I really am ready to seriously date and wondering how I'm going to get Connor's face to stop popping into my head.

15

CONNOR

"Couldn't we have just bought these pre-made?" I ask, lifting my sad excuse for a wreath from where I sit in the middle of Tori's living room.

"Nope. I couldn't order that many in bulk, so we'll have to settle for making our own. Come on, that looks great!" She offers a broad smile, pointing to my pathetic creation.

"You're just saying that so I won't leave you to make them all by yourself."

She ponders my statement with a blank stare before tilting her head. "Maybe," she admits. "But I think our guests will appreciate a handmade wreath, even if it is terrible."

"So you do think it's terrible."

"That's not what I said."

"But it's what you were implying."

"Perhaps," she says after a brief pause, the corner of her

mouth lifting up into a smirk. "Okay, fine, I just don't want you to bail and leave me alone to drown in this sea of foliage."

Even though I know she's talking about making wreaths, I let myself wonder if maybe a small part of her likes having me around. If she enjoys being together as much as I do.

For what seems like the millionth time today, I mentally clear my head and try to shift my attention to work and the task at hand before I get myself flustered. My mind has been wandering more and more to thoughts of Tori, and each time it does, it makes me a little more confused and anxious. Maybe even a little bit nauseated. What does it all mean? And how do I get myself to snap out of it and focus? This is why I haven't bothered with dating—it's distracting.

It doesn't help that I've noticed how something about her has shifted too—ever since the parade. I can't pinpoint it, but the way she looks at me is different than the way she used to. Like when she holds my stare for a second too long. It's obvious that there's something going on behind those eyes of hers. Something that she's clearly feeling but not saying out loud.

The email notification on my phone breaks me out of my spiraling thoughts, and I gently set my half-done wreath on the floor to reach into my pocket for it.

"Is that our buyer? Coming in with a full-ask offer? The one that's going to make us a lot of money and give us the satisfaction of beating Rich?" Tori rambles, her eyes playfully dancing with excitement.

I chuckle. "Unfortunately, no. But it was an email from a fellow agent, letting me know he'll be sending me an offer shortly for my listing on Lima St."

"Oh, that's exciting!" Tori flashes me a grin as I set my phone next to me, waiting for it to ring.

"I mean, it's peanuts compared to Makana Manor, but you won't hear me complaining. How are your other listings doing?" I ask.

"Pretty good." She focuses down on her wreath, tucking her thick hair behind her ear. "Managed to close a deal yesterday morning at 1.1 million, and then I have a listing appointment with a potential client tomorrow. So not bad."

"Not bad at all." I'm about to say more, but my ringing phone interrupts with a call from the agent.

"Do you mind if I take this outside?" I ask, coming to stand.

"Not at all. Good luck."

I dip my head and unintentionally hold her stare for an extra beat before I turn and reach the balcony.

"This is Connor," I say into the phone, shutting the sliding door closed behind me, feeling a surge of confidence and adrenaline pulse through me, as it always does when I shift into work mode.

"Connor, it's Roger. I take it that you saw my email?"

"I did. My client will be happy to hear that we've got a solid offer on the table. What do you have for me?" I watch as the palm trees by the pool below sway with the wind, creating a muffled whistling sound in the air.

"We're coming in at seven-hundred-fifty thousand. All cash. Thirty-day close."

"I'll present the offer, but you know there's quite a big jump between that number and the listing price of seven-ninety-nine."

"Just get back to me with his response. We'll go from there and see what we can work out," he says kindly. Negotiations are commonplace in real estate, and there is usually a little bit of back and forth before an offer is accepted, so this is par for the course when it comes to making a deal.

I call up my client right away. "Jonah, good news. We've got an offer on the table. Seven-hundred-fifty-thousand, which is decent, but I'm confident that I can get him to come up."

"Okay, see what you can do, I guess. I mean, we're desperate to get out and move on from this property, so I'd be happy with the offer the way it is, but obviously, the higher the number, the better," he tells me. "Go ahead and work your magic."

"You got it. Keep your phone on you. I'll be in touch shortly."

After some back and forth between the buyer's agent and Jonah, we successfully come to an agreement at seven-hundred-seventy-five thousand dollars and a plan for me to get the paperwork going as soon as I can. The familiar rush of excitement and satisfaction that comes with closing a deal of any size pumps through my veins as I slip my phone in my pocket and slide the door open.

"Judging by your smile, I'd say it's good news?" Tori asks from the same spot on the floor.

"Made a deal," I confirm with a nod, the smile lingering on my face.

"Yay! We have to celebrate," she says, jumping up, looking back at me as she walks to the kitchen. "Do you like white wine?"

"I do, but we don't have to celebrate," I say, although I'm already following behind her. "I usually don't do much."

"Let me guess." She peels the paper wrapping off the top of a bottle and pulls a wine opener out of a drawer. "Your post-deal celebrations consist of you sitting alone on your couch in your cold, empty house."

"That was harsh." I happily grab two wine glasses from the hanging rack under the cabinet and set them on the counter, completely ignoring her jab.

"Sorry," she says sheepishly.

"But also accurate," I admit. I watch as she fills the glasses with wine.

"Here." She hands me a glass and then says in a gentle voice, "You're worth celebrating, Connor."

The way she says my name makes it noticeably harder to

breathe, and I can't pull my stare away from hers as we clink our glasses together.

"Thank you, Tori," I say quietly. The intensity of her eyes is alluring and all-encompassing before it just barely crosses the line of being too much. I shift my gaze down at my glass as I take a sip and then clear my throat.

She places her palms flat against the countertop of the island behind her and hoists herself up to sit on top of it. I stay where I'm at, cemented like a statue next to her, hyper-aware of her closeness and the heat radiating off her body. My heart feels like it's pounding against my chest, ramping up even faster with every second just by being this close to her, so I find a welcome distraction in the pile of mail nearby.

"Wow, you have a lot of cards," I say, picking the top one off the stack. It's an older couple with their arms around each other, smiling wide in front of a golf course sign in Phoenix, Arizona.

"Yeah, I don't know what to do with all of them," she says quietly.

"Is this more than what you normally get?" I ask, picking up another one that says *Happy Holidays from Kissimmee, FL*, hoping she doesn't mind that I'm essentially going through her mail.

"It's a long story." She huffs a soft laugh, taking another sip of wine. "Elliot thinks I'm a charity case. He signed me up for this program at his school where people from around the world can send you holiday greetings."

"Why would he do that?" My head tilts to the right, meeting her gaze that once again takes a hold of me. Neither one of us moves or breaks the stare.

"Because he thinks I'm lonely," she cracks out in a broken whisper, clearly also feeling affected by whatever energy is passing between us. Her eyes search mine back and forth, and I can see her chest rising and falling with deeper breaths than just a moment ago.

I slide barely an inch closer to her, with hesitation in my approach. When she doesn't shake her head or look away, I somehow find the boldness to move even closer.

My heart is pounding wildly, and my brain feels cloudy, filled with racing thoughts and uncertainties, but my body reacts as if it has a mind of its own. I can't force myself to stop moving, her eyes luring my whole body in slowly like a magnet until I'm standing in between her legs, her face directly in front of mine.

She breaks the stare by dipping her eyes to my lips and rolling her own. I place my hands on the cold counter on either side of her, leaning in slightly.

"Are you?" I ask quietly, bringing her eyes back up to mine. "Lonely?"

The way her expression softens, as if I just found a part of her that not everyone sees, tells me the answer to my question.

"How can I be lonely?" she whispers back with a forced smile, trying to cover up any vulnerability. "You've met my family. I have more than enough people around me."

"That's not what I asked." My voice comes out low and gravelly, wiping the smile right off her face. The connection is intoxicating, drawing my head forward.

"Are you lonely?" I ask again, hovering right over her mouth.

She doesn't answer, but instead closes what's left of the gap between us, pressing her lips to mine. Immediately, any nerves that I was holding onto fade away as I completely melt into her. She runs her fingers softly up the outsides of my arms, leaving a trail of electricity in their wake, then clasping her hands together at the base of my neck. Moving my hands to cup her outer thighs, I press as far as I can into her and against the island.

After a few moments of being completely caught up in a high that I don't think I've ever experienced before, a soft sigh escapes her throat, and the sound seems to awaken us from whatever haze we were just lost in. All of the reasons why this is a bad idea start flashing through my head, causing me to tense up, and I separate from her, putting space between us.

"Uh, I'm so sorry," I mumble, trying to slow down the rambling thoughts in my head and the effect of her kiss that still lingers through my body. What were we thinking? What happened to no work flings? And where the hell did that confidence come from?

She shakes her head from side to side, eyes widening as if she just woke up from a trance. "Oh my gosh, I don't know where that came from." She hops down off the island and walks the other way around it, putting even more distance between us. I try and gauge her reaction, but her expression isn't giving anything away.

"I mean, neither one of us wants to have a thing with a coworker, right?" I ask her hesitantly when she stops on the other side of the island, cautiously eyeing me, and I have a hard time keeping my eyes away from her lips.

She emphatically nods. "Yes. Yes, absolutely. That was stupid. And should absolutely never happen again."

A small wave of relief washes over me, thankful that we're on the same page. As absolutely amazing as that kiss was, I know that I can't deal with anything messy right now. One hundred percent of my focus needs to be on work. And kissing my coworker has messy written all over it—no matter how attracted I am to her.

"Agreed," I say. "So…we're good?"

She taps her hands on the island. "Yes. Perfect. Fantastic."

I let out a small laugh at her insistence but appreciate that she isn't making our momentary lapse in judgment awkward for either of us.

"Should we get back to the wreaths?" I ask softly, wanting to make sure that we really are okay and that she's comfortable with me staying.

"Yes. Good idea." She nods her head firmly.

I follow her back into the living room, where I spend the rest of the evening crafting miserable-looking wreaths and trying unsuccessfully to forget the way her body felt when it was pressed to mine.

16

TORI

"As you can see, no stone has been left unturned with this property. They've truly thought of every amenity that you'd ever need," I tell Sarah, my out-of-town potential client, as I pull open the automatic retractable doors that lead to the outdoor pool area at Makana Manor. She reaches for her black sunglasses that are on top of her head to slide them on, then smooths her stick-straight blonde hair as we step outside.

"Wow," the high-powered businesswoman breathes, both of our heels clicking against the concrete patio as we walk toward the pool. "This is remarkable. Truly. I don't mean to brag, but we have vacation homes in Aspen and in Puerto Vallarta and trust me, I know luxury. This property would definitely take the cake for us if we add this to our roster. I can see us vacationing here already."

"Do you think your husband and kids would approve?" I ask, neatly folding my hand over my other wrist, trying to contain the small buzz of adrenaline that's running underneath the surface of my skin from the energy of this showing.

"They would. I'm only here for two days—I flew in just to look at this house in person—but I think I'll need to bring my husband back so he can see it for himself. I'd like to make a move on it quickly if he approves. How much interest have you had in it?"

"Quite a bit." I only stretch the truth slightly. There has certainly been interest, but the interest always fades away once the topic of price comes up. Something tells me that the price won't be a deterrent with these clients, though. "How soon do you plan to make a trip back? We have a holiday gala open house planned for next week. If you can make it work, you should try and be back in town so you can come to it. It will be all decked out for the party, so you'll get a good sense of what it would be like to host a holiday gathering."

"Oh." Her eyes perk up, and I can almost see her brain working as she thinks. "That sounds magnificent. Actually, do you mind if I call my husband now? I'd like to run it by him if you don't mind? I won't take long."

"Not at all. Take your time. I'll be out here when you're ready." I walk leisurely around the perimeter of the pool while Sarah goes inside the house to make her phone call. A nearby wind chime sings from the rustling of the wind that's swaying the palm trees above my head. I sit on the edge of a lounge chair, tucking my dress under my legs, and scroll through the unopened emails on my phone. The sun feels warm against the back of my neck as I attempt to focus on them. But in reality, it's taking everything in me to not think about the other major thing that's been adding to my adrenaline today—Connor. And what happened in my kitchen last night.

To say that kiss was incredible would be an understatement. It sent me into a fog that I still haven't fully emerged from almost an entire day later. Never-ending thoughts and emotions have been constantly running through my mind today, as much as I've been trying to push them to the side. What did the kiss mean? Does Connor have feelings for me too? Clearly there's a chemistry there between us—our kiss being exhibit A—but how long has he been wanting to kiss me?

I'm glad we're both on the same page about putting our professionalism above anything else, and I still stand by that, but that doesn't mean that the whole encounter will be easy to forget. Quite the opposite, actually, if how frazzled I've been ever since is any indicator. Of course, it's just my luck that the hottest, most chemistry-laden kiss of my life was with someone who's completely off-limits.

As much as I tried to act normally after the kiss, I was hyper-aware of his presence in my living room for the rest of the evening. Every move he made just had me more zoned in on him than the last. That patheticness is exactly why I've purposefully put some distance between us today, using meetings for other listings as an excuse to avoid the office and seeing him face-to-face. Connor and I have only connected via text message today —and very minimally at that. It's weird to not see him at all since we've been spending so much time together, but I just don't think I can trust my resolve around him right now and don't feel like testing that theory yet.

My phone buzzes with an incoming text message, and I open it to see a picture that Quinn just sent over. It's a selfie of her with the Parthenon monument in the background. I smile, happy that she's enjoying her trip to Greece, and promise myself that I'll call her later.

"Sorry about that," Sarah says, sliding her phone back into her purse as she approaches me. "He's as excited as I am. In fact, he's looking into flights as we speak for us to come back. I'd love to be able to show it to him in a private showing with you as well as come to your gala—if you'll have us, of course."

"Absolutely." I stand and offer a smile. "We would love to have you."

"Excellent. I have a really good feeling about this place, Tori. It feels really good." She says it in a way that tells me while she is excited, she means business first and foremost, not letting too much emotion come through.

"That makes me so glad," I tell her. "I'm happy to be of assistance in your search for a vacation home."

"Thank you. Oh, before we leave, I'd love to check out the stretch of beach by the water if you wouldn't mind showing me?" she asks hopefully.

"Not at all. Right this way." I lead her to the set of concrete stairs near the left-hand side of the pool area and gently lift a stray tree branch that's hanging over the middle of the stairs, pausing long enough to let her pass through. We get to the bottom step, and I slip off my strappy heels before stepping onto the warm sand that juts right up to the step. Sarah does the same with her own heels, and with shoes hanging from our hands, we walk through the sand toward the ocean.

"So you have one-hundred-twenty-three feet of private beach that starts at that line right over there and runs all the way to where that shrub line starts if you can see that," I tell her, pointing out the property line. You can see neighbors down a little bit on both sides of the property, but the majority of the houses' exteriors are hidden behind trees and fenced in backyards, truly creating a secluded atmosphere on the beach.

"Okay. Wow. It's so quiet," she comments, making a slow circle.

"It's a very quiet neighborhood," I agree. "Not a whole lot of hustle and bustle nearby, and this is your own personal slice of tranquility right here. Imagine the bonfires you could have out here and the beach games. Not to mention the swimming and other water activities—right from your backyard."

The waves crash onto the shore as the wind gusts gently

around us, causing my hair to lift and swirl in the air. I slide my sunglasses on, attempting to block the beaming sun that is shining down on us from where it sits in the sky over the water.

"Absolutely picturesque," she says as we take a few slow steps along the edge of the water before turning to gaze at the backyard view of the sprawling estate. The expansive property is a beautiful mix of thick, strong lines of the outer structure mixed with a whimsical flair from the greenery and soft lights that fill in any empty space surrounding it, making it appear grand and majestic.

"Someone will be the lucky homeowner soon," I point out gently.

"It'll be me if I have anything to say about it," she says firmly, a confidence to her voice that has me hoping her husband will feel the same. We walk slowly back inside, enjoying the warmth of the air, and I allow myself to wonder if Sarah just might be our buyer after all.

17

____

CONNOR

"Yes, the closing will be at nine a.m. on Friday. I'll meet you at the title office. See you then." I hang up the phone to end my conversation with my client, then become so preoccupied with skimming through an offer letter document that I hardly notice the gentleman mere inches from me as I step through the sliding doors of the assisted living facility.

"Excuse me, sorry," I apologize, weaving through the swarm of people that are gathered in the main area, festive music filling the room at an almost obscene volume.

A sign that reads *Santa Hats and Cinema,* the name of this annual holiday event, hangs above the fireplace, where garland and mini Christmas trees sit on top of the mantel. After rounding the corner, I approach the craft tables and immediately zero in on Tori, who's sitting in between my grandparents and who I've successfully managed to avoid up until right now. Stopping in my tracks, I swallow down the sudden thickness that grips my throat, and I feel a nervous energy slowly start to ramp up under the surface of my skin. I was not expecting her to be here, of all places, this morning. Although, we didn't check in at all earlier, so I'm not sure where I figured she would be—but certainly not here, wedged between my grandparents.

She glances up, and when we lock eyes, I push through the nervous energy and pull half of my mouth up into a smile and give a timid wave.

"Hey," I say to the general table as I approach, but I'm unable to look at anyone else but Tori.

"Oh, Connor, dear," Grandma says, fluttering her fingers in greeting. "Have a seat. Hurry, you need to get started on your Santa hat. The movie starts in twenty minutes!"

"Sure thing," I reply, still not releasing Tori's stare. "What are you doing here?" I ask, hoping my tone comes out as being curious and not accusatory.

"I hope it's okay that I'm here. Betty invited me," she says quietly, an innocent smile playing on her lips. I nod, sliding my hands into my shorts pockets in an attempt to compose myself.

"Of course she did," I mumble to myself, moving closer and pulling out a chair next to Grandpa.

"Grandma already started you off by tracing your name," he says, placing a hat in front of me.

"Wonderful." I pick up a tube of green puff paint because I know the path of least resistance is to go ahead and decorate a darn hat. No point in fighting it. Although, I'm hoping I can look past this buzzing energy enough to concentrate on the hat. I can't tell if I'm feeling this way from nerves or if this is simply how I react to being near Tori now.

"Your grandparents were just giving me relationship advice and tips for us to apply to our life together." The laugh that Tori's trying so hard to hold back filters out with her words, and I sigh, noting the amusement dancing in her eyes. I'm glad she's able to find the humor in the situation, and it helps to lessen some of my own nerves. But the small hint of vulnerability—the same one I saw in her kitchen—isn't lost on me.

"Again, Grandma, we're not—" I start.

"I was telling her all about how Louie and I made a commitment a long time ago to spend quality time together. No matter how busy life gets, you should always make being together a priority. Although, to be honest, in our young years, I didn't realize that we'd end up here."

"Now, all we do is spend time together. I can't get away from her," Grandpa jokes.

"And aren't we lucky to still have each other?" Grandma leans in front of Tori toward Grandpa, who meets her halfway for a kiss.

"You two are so sweet," Tori gushes, crinkling her brows in amusement when they sit back down.

"Snowflakes, please," I say as politely as I can, trying to maneuver the conversation in a different direction.

"Sure thing," Grandma says, lifting the bowl of felt snowflakes. "I'll also hand you some jingle bells to glue on— those are always fun."

Much to my surprise, we spend several minutes making hats without any more mention of Tori and me or relationships in general. Although, that hasn't stopped me from stealing glances and accidentally making eye contact with her from across the table a few times, each instance making my stomach dip ever so slightly and ultimately helping to melt away any nervousness that was lingering.

"All done with mine. I think I'll grab some hot chocolate before we head in for the movie," Tori says, addressing my grandparents. "Can I get you two a cup?"

"That would be wonderful, sweetheart. Connor, this one's a keeper," Grandma says.

"I'll come with you," I offer, much preferring Tori's company to the grilling I would inevitably receive with her gone from the table. I let her pass first, trying to fight the urge to get as close to her as I can while we walk to the hot cocoa bar that's set up along the outer wall. There's a short line of people waiting, so I lean somewhat awkwardly against the wall while we wait.

"Sorry for not telling you I was coming today," Tori says slowly, the uncertain expression on her face matching my own clouded thoughts. "I didn't want to let Betty down after she invited me. She seemed so excited. But truthfully, I didn't know if you'd want me here after the other day."

"Tori," I start, cutting through my awkward nerves. I don't like seeing her flustered, and I know that it's best for both of us if we just address what happened. We've both resorted to avoiding each other ever since, and I'm not proud of doing that. But I'm still not quite clear on what to say to her.

"It's okay," she says with a shrug, probably sensing my discomfort at the topic. "We don't have to talk about it."

"No, I think we should." A sudden determination to hash this out hits me hard. "Clearly, neither of us has handled this the best way, so I think we should get it all out on the table so we can acknowledge it and move on."

"Okay." She nods, grabbing two cups from the corner of the table as the line moves forward. "You go first," she says with the beginnings of a playful smile before turning to fill them with the hot cocoa that's in the crockpot.

After letting out a sigh and grabbing two more cups, we start making our way down the table that's filled with every different kind of topping you could think of—candy cane bits, toffee crumbles, white chocolate sprinkles, and mini marshmallows, to name a few.

"Obviously, there's an…attraction between us," I start out awkwardly, wondering why she left me to start when she knows this stuff is pure torture for me. She nods, flicking her gaze up to meet mine, the small flame of intensity behind them telling me she's remembering our kiss.

"But neither of us have ever wanted to entertain dating in the workplace, right?" I again point out the obvious roadblock to anything more happening between us and use the mini scoop to pour some toffee crumbles into my hot chocolate. I wait patiently, eager to hear her genuine thoughts.

"Right," she says slowly, "because we are both professionals, and our careers mean a lot to us. Dating could cause us to lose focus and potentially ruin our work environment if things don't work out." Something about the way she tucks a strand of hair back behind her ear has me searching my brain for any reason or excuse to prove why that's a dumb theory.

"Correct." My agreement causes a tiny flash of disappointment across her face, and I hold onto that with all my might. "But…"

"But?" A hint of hope glimmers just slightly across her face as my brain works overtime. Can we make something work? Am I capable of juggling both work and a relationship, especially with my coworker? Will I have the confidence to take that step with Tori? I don't have a definitive answer, but I do know that the mere idea of it all happening with Tori makes me want to at least try.

"Here's my take," I finally say. "I think part of why we're both so successful is because we know how to micromanage and prioritize when needed. Do you think maybe we could apply those skills to this situation and be capable of not letting whatever happens between us affect our work?"

"Perhaps." Her eyebrows lift as she instantly perks up, and it fuels me on.

"Can we keep the two separate? When we're working, we stay focused on the tasks at hand, and when we're doing… whatever else…we don't focus on work?"

She rolls her lips in concentration, thinking it over. "I think we're both mature enough to handle that," she says, biting back a growing smile as she sprays some whipped cream onto the tops of her two cups. I grab the caramel sauce to drizzle on both of mine. We step off to the side to let others in the line come through, ending up in a quiet corner at the far end of the room. The piping-hot beverages warm my hands in the air conditioning they have blasting in here.

"I mean, why fight it, right? If we can do this the right way?" she asks, her eyes dancing playfully as they meet mine.

"Exactly," I say, a smile tugging at the corner of my mouth. "Let's test the waters and see how it goes. If it gets too hard, or work starts to slip, then we stop immediately."

"Okay," she agrees quickly.

"And I promise to not hate you after we go down in flames."

She laughs. "Same to you. And I promise to not let whatever happens affect either of our careers in a negative way."

"So we have a deal?" I ask, both anticipation and apprehension swirling in my stomach.

"We have a deal." She nods in confidence.

"Then let me take you out on a date." The words come out fast and sound foreign, like they're coming from someone else the second they slip out, but even so, not a single part of me wants to take them back.

"A date?" Her grin is incredibly distracting, but I force my gaze away from her mouth and back up to her eyes.

"An official date," I confirm, not having the slightest clue what we'll do but knowing with certainty that I'll do my best to come up with a date that she deserves.

"That sounds lovely."

With one last shared smile, we finally walk down the hallway to the rec room, where my grandparents are already seated in a row of folding chairs toward the front of the room that are angled at the projection screen. I slide next to Grandpa, and Tori sits in the chair next to me. We pass them their cups of hot cocoa as they hand us our Santa hats, which we promptly put on. As the lights start to dim, Tori peers over at me with a small smile.

"To testing the waters," I whisper, holding eye contact, lifting my cup.

"To testing the waters." She gently touches her cup to mine, and there we sit for the next two hours, wearing scratchy hats and sipping lukewarm hot cocoa while watching *It's a Wonderful Life* in the assisted living facility. I try my best to ignore the nervous energy in the back of my mind and choose to focus on enjoying the moment and looking forward to what's to come.

18

———

TORI

"We're really doing this?" Emily asks excitedly when I open my door, her eyes beaming. "We're going on a date with Connor?"

"We are," I say, letting her all the way in, wondering if I could somehow convince her to come with me so that I can channel some of her enthusiasm all night. Apprehension about this date has been ramping up ever since I left the office about an hour ago. Not that I'm not excited about it, because I definitely am. I think I'm just questioning and hoping that we're making the right decision with moving forward. The last thing I want to do is break the solid work relationship that we've formed.

"Okay, show me your options," she says, walking past me down the hall to my bedroom, where Grace is already sifting through my closet. I sent an emergency text earlier to my sisters when I left work, after I had a sudden panic attack on the walk home about what I should wear tonight, and requested backup. These emergency date texts are typical for us, and they always lead to whatever sisters are available jumping in to help. Emily and Grace are my support team tonight.

"We've got this green romper," Grace says, pulling it out and tossing it on my bed and then pointing to the other options that are already lying across it. "That black jumper and that white sundress so far."

"What are you doing on your date? How fancy do you need to be?" Emily asks, jumping right in next to Grace, taking a pantsuit out to inspect.

"I'm not sure, actually," I say with a shrug, sitting on the edge of my bed. "He didn't give me too many details. He just said he'd pick me up around six."

"Okay, so we've got nothing to work with." Emily pulls out a navy-blue dress. "How about this?"

"No, I just wore that two days ago to a closing and then the office after that, so Connor has already seen me in it."

"Hasn't Connor seen you in most of these outfits, then?" Grace asks, placing a hand on her hip.

"Yes," I groan, falling back onto my bed, my arms spreading out with my palms up. "That's my problem. I didn't have time to go shopping for something new."

"Okay, drama queen." Emily pulls on my wrist until I'm sitting straight up. "You're not allowed to complain when you have a closet full of mostly designer clothing, okay?" She smiles sweetly.

"Why don't you try some of these on so we can see what they look like?" Grace points to the three options on my bed.

"Fine," I grumble, taking the three hangers with me to the bathroom. I try the green romper on first, immediately hating it and taking it off without even coming out of the bathroom.

"Romper's a no," I call through the door and then pull on the black jumper before walking back into my room.

"Oh, I like that one," Emily says, making a twirling motion with her finger. I spin around slowly, lifting my arms out wide.

"How do you feel in it?" Grace asks.

"Meh," I say.

"Then it's a no. Try on the last one," she says.

Back in the bathroom, I pull on the white sundress, already liking it the most so far. It has a sweetheart neckline with thin spaghetti straps, is tight around my ribcage, and then loosely hangs down to my calves with an open slit in the front.

"I can already tell this is a winner," Emily says. "You look a little less grouchy in it."

"I do like this one," I admit, feeling slightly more optimistic. "And it's been a while since I've worn it."

"Perfect. Now what are we doing with your hair?" Grace asks, trailing behind me as I head back to the bathroom.

"I'll probably leave it down. Throw a couple more curls in it." The three of us squeeze into my bathroom, where I plug my curling iron in and grab my mascara out of the clear acrylic makeup organizer that sits on my vanity.

"So why are you nervous?" Emily asks. "Your text gave the impression that you were spiraling a little bit."

"I kind of was," I admit. "I'm just really nervous about this not working out—and what that would mean for my work life."

"I get that," Grace says. "But, Tori, I've seen the way he looks at you. You have nothing to worry about, trust me."

I can't help the smile that spreads slowly across my face. I can picture the exact look that she's talking about because it's a look that I haven't seen on him before until recently. It's the way he sometimes looks at me like he can't believe I'm real. Like he thinks I'm the most captivating woman in the world. He also looks at me with a blank stare that borders on annoyance, but that look also makes me smile.

"Oh, I saw that at the parade. Scott doesn't even look at me like that anymore," Emily laughs.

"You definitely need a taupe lip moment," Grace says, pulling a tube of lipstick out and handing it to me.

"I think I can get myself ready now, guys. Crisis averted," I say, excitement starting to overpower any nerves that I was experiencing. I remind myself that it's Connor we're talking about here. We get along so well with each other and have always communicated well, so why should this be any different? I start to feel a bit more confident that we'll be able to navigate this together—however it ends up.

"Sorry, we're committed now," Emily says, completely unfazed, not moving a muscle.

I apply the lipstick and dab on a little bit of blush before grabbing the curling iron.

"You look gorg," Grace says when I finish my hair and step back to assess the final look.

"Do you feel good?" Emily asks me.

"I do." I nod, feeling butterflies ramping up in my stomach. I feel another sudden surge of excitement. "I feel great, actually. Thanks for your help, guys."

"Of course," Grace says as we file out of the bathroom and down the hall toward the kitchen. "Let's hope this one's a keeper. You deserve at least a decent date after your last few."

"No kidding," Emily chimes in. "Remember when that one guy insisted that you split the bill after he ordered the most expensive steak on the menu? And two different kinds of dessert!"

"Or the one who showed up forty minutes late, claiming he had a nervous stomach?" Grace asks with a laugh.

"Yes, unfortunately, I do remember. That's why I took a little dating break," I say, slipping the tube of lipstick into my purse that's lying on the kitchen counter. Grace and Emily slide onto two of the chairs that rest under the island, clearly not in a hurry to leave. I raise my brows, throwing them a questioning look.

"Are you going to join me on the date too?" I ask.

"Can we? We'd stay far enough back that you wouldn't even see us," Emily says hopefully.

"No." I laugh, leaning over to rest my forearms across the countertop.

"Ooh, are these the Christmas cards?" Grace asks, referencing the stack in front of her. I'm not sure if she's genuinely interested or if she's just stalling. I don't bother answering, as now they've both dug into the pile of cards and are inspecting them.

"Oh my gosh, cute. Look at this sweet family from New Jersey," Emily says, flipping the card over. Again, I don't entertain them, knowing they're just buying time. Instead, I throw them both a smile.

"You can go now," I say as sweetly as possible.

"Aw man, can't we stay until he gets here?" Grace pouts, setting the cards back in the pile.

"Absolutely not. He'll be here in twenty minutes," I say, moving closer and waving my hands to shoo them out of their chairs.

"Fine," Emily grumbles, coming to a stand. "Make sure you text us updates, though, okay?"

They slip their sandals on in my doorway as I wait patiently, holding the door open for them.

"I will text you tomorrow," I say before holding out my free arm for a hug.

"Okay, bye! Have so much fun!" Emily says, squeezing me in a quick side hug and moving into the hallway. Grace comes in next for a hug.

"It'll be great," she says into my ear before joining Emily. "And you look incredible."

With a smile, I watch as they make their way down the hallway toward the elevator. I blow out a steady sigh and head back into my condo to wait for Connor.

19

TORI

"So…there's a crab and steak dinner as well as live entertainment all included in this sunset cruise," Connor explains, his hands fumbling to slide his phone in the pocket of his khaki shorts, nerves almost palpably rolling off him as we walk down the beach, skirting around a group of people lying on beach towels. It's obvious that he's been stuck in his head about being out on an official date with me ever since he picked me up, judging by his fidgety hands and hesitant words.

"No personal chef or boat reservation just for two?" I tease him, feeling only mildly bad that I find his discomfort so entertaining.

"No. Is that what you wanted? Shoot, I should have done that," he mumbles, scratching at the back of his head.

"I'm kidding," I laugh, grabbing his forearm, which stiffens slightly under my touch. I've seen Connor get flustered around women before, and I know that he's not super confident in this aspect of his life, but I don't like the fact that he feels uncomfortable around me.

"Oh," he laughs nervously. "I think there's all-you-can-eat breadsticks too."

"You had me at breadsticks."

He looks like he's maybe about to say something, but his phone rings in his pocket, and all of a sudden, he's spiraling into an even bigger ball of nerves. He stops himself from reaching for it, but I can see that he's holding on by a thread here. I'm suddenly grateful that I had my sisters to help ease my own nerves earlier, and I know that I'm definitely feeling more put together than he is right now.

"Hey, wait," I say gently, coming to a stop, thankful that we seem to have made it to a slightly less busy stretch of beach. He makes it another step before turning to look back at me.

"Yeah? Are you okay?" he asks, concern flashing across his face as he gives me a once-over.

"I'm fine," I reassure, stepping close enough that the fresh yet woody scent of his cologne hangs in the air, momentarily distracting me. "Let's just take a breather for a second. Okay?"

He nods, looking down the beach where the boat is just starting to let people on. His breaths are short and shallow, and his hands are fidgety.

"Look at me," I say, grabbing his hand tentatively. He slides his sunglasses on top of his head and takes my hand, connecting his eyes with mine. When they do, I see the slightest reprieve from whatever he's been feeling, and the cloudiness just barely drifts away. His black polo shirt makes his green eyes seem even more intense, sucking me in.

"It's just me," I say quietly, keeping my eyes pinned on his, wanting to connect and get through to him. He holds my stare and gives the slightest nod in return.

"Are you okay?" I ask him the same question he asked me

moments ago. His response is rapidly nodding his head while rolling his lips together.

"Yeah, yeah. All good. As long as you're still good," he spits out.

I consider the cruise we're about to embark on, which I know will be full of people, crowded and busy. An idea springs to my mind, and I can't help the small rush of excitement that washes over me. "I have an idea."

His eyes narrow, scanning over my face.

"Do you trust me?" I ask.

"Uh…" He shrugs, unsure of what to say.

"Let's not go on the boat," I say decisively, dropping my purse right on the sand, and it lands with a thud.

"What do you mean?"

"Drop your phone and wallet," I instruct, tossing my sandals next to my purse, feeling his confused stare burning into me.

"Listen." I face him head-on. "I know you went through the trouble of planning a lovely date, and I appreciate it so much. Really, I do." I push my lips together before flashing him a grin. "But let's skip it."

"Skip it?" His eyebrows fly up, his eyes widening.

"Skip it." I hold my palm out flat and wait for him to hesitantly place his phone and wallet in my hand. Once he does, I place them gently on top of my purse. I grab his hand again and use my other hand to hike up my sundress.

"Come on!" I say, pulling him along as I start jogging toward the ocean, adrenaline surging through me.

"What are we doing? Tori!" he shouts from a half-stride behind me, but there's no resistance or pulling on my arm, meaning he's right there with me, so I surge forward, the sand flying up behind me as I run.

"Loosening up!" I yell back with a laugh. When my feet hit the water, I let out a squeal and drop Connor's hand to use both of mine to hike my dress even higher. The waves surge against my legs, and I push against them, continuing on until I'm waist-deep. When I turn around to see where he ended up, I find Connor mere inches from me, fully submerged in the water up to his head as he swims past me, fancy date clothes and all.

Bending my knees, I sink until the water touches the tips of my shoulders. I don't trust my swimming capabilities with this dress on, so I keep my toes touching the sand, not wanting to go out any farther. Connor floats closer until we're face to face, and I'm relieved to see that he doesn't look flustered at all. There's no trace of the anxiety or tension that was consuming him just moments before. As if the ocean just completely washed it away.

"Are you telling me that this is all I had to plan for you to be happy?" His eyes twinkle, and I zero in on the way the water reflects in them. "An impromptu, fully dressed dip in the ocean?"

"What can I say? I'm easy to please." He shakes his head at my response as my legs get tangled in the bottom of my dress, and I lower one arm to try and adjust the fabric, but a wave causes me to stumble backward, my arms spreading out to keep me afloat. My head barely stays above the water.

"Here," he says softly. "Let me help." A strong hand finds my elbow and effortlessly pulls me in until I'm brushing up against his stomach, and his other arm wraps around my back, holding me afloat. My chest tightens, and I watch as his eyes scan down to my mouth, causing a flutter to run wild in my stomach.

"Now you don't look like a drowning rat," he mumbles, attempting to tease me, but it comes off flat. He seems to be as distracted by our closeness as I am.

"At least I'm a pretty drowned rat," I whisper, completely focused on him, feeling his arm tighten around my back as I bring my head closer to his. He nods, bringing his eyes back up to meet mine.

"The prettiest," he murmurs at the very last moment before he brings his lips to mine. My stomach flips as I bring my arms around his neck, pressing myself flat against his stomach. The tips of his fingers grip the fabric of my dress at my waist, bunching it into his fist against my side. His other hand trails up my back and rests at the base of my neck. I bring my hands around both sides of his neck, just under his ears, and allow myself to fully get lost in this kiss, especially since our last one was cut short.

A wave splashes against our shoulders, spraying water on our faces, causing us to separate before I'm ready to, but neither of us loosens our grips. My thumbs move simultaneously, grazing the skin underneath his ears, running them along each side of his jawline before I slide my fingers further around his head, interlacing them at the base of his neck.

One of his hands runs down my spine, along my hips, and when it reaches my leg, I follow his gentle tugging by lifting both of my legs around his waist, joining my ankles behind him. His hand comes to rest under my legs, holding me up as I move my head closer to bring my lips back to his. He presses back against me firmly, opening his mouth to urge a deeper kiss, which I respond to readily. My stomach dips as I'm fully aware of the stark contrast between how confident he is when we're close like this versus how nervous he was just a few moments ago on the beach. It's like he's as lost in the moment as I am, no concern of outside pressures or thoughts.

When we separate, a sly smile plays on his lips, and I try to get my heart rate to return to a normal speed. We spend a few seconds immersed in the moment and in each other's stare. Then, off in the distance, a boat travels by, faint music drifting to shore.

"There goes our boat," he says, glancing over his shoulder.

"Yeah. I think this was a much better idea, though," I say.

"Much. But you are getting kind of heavy." He laughs when I

hit him with a slap on his shoulder. I wiggle my way out of his grip, even though he attempts to pull me back in.

"Alright, let's head in," he says, releasing me altogether and moving toward shore.

"The burning question is, what are you going to feed me for dinner now?"

20

CONNOR

"How's your poke bowl?" I ask, taking a bite from my own food container in my hands.

"Amazing," Tori replies, politely covering her food-filled mouth with the back of her hand.

I had spent the entire day leading up to our date worrying about making it perfect and enjoyable for her, and yet, here we are, doing nothing that I planned. We're nestled under a group of palm trees in a little corner on the beach—the food truck where we spontaneously grabbed food is visible just up the shoreline. Still-damp clothes cling to our bodies, and grainy sand covers our feet. It's not even close to anything grand or extraordinary, yet somehow, it's okay. I don't know why, but it feels more than okay with her.

"Alright." Tori sets her bowl next to her in the sand and angles toward me, criss-crossing her legs. "So let's see. This is technically our first date. What questions should I ask to get to know you better?"

"My favorite color is blue," I throw out with a shrug.

"That's a start," she says with a nod. "Oh! What's your favorite meal? Breakfast, lunch, or dinner?"

"Dinner. Hands down."

"And what's your favorite food to eat for dinner?"

"Nothing beats a good steak and mashed potatoes. What about you?" I ask.

"I'd have to say breakfast is my favorite," she replies after taking a second to think. "And I love a good quiche or blueberry pancakes."

"Would you rather cook or order in?" I ask.

"I don't cook a whole lot. It's easier to just grab a meal on the go."

"Same," I agree. She scoots a little bit closer, and the only thing I feel is happy and comfortable—maybe slightly buzzed from being so close. But it's apparent that there's absolutely no sign of my nerves from earlier. Nothing holds me back as I scoot the rest of the way until we're pressed into each other's sides. I'm not sure if it's because we were friends first, or if it's just because it's her specifically, but there have been so many moments like this tonight when this is all somehow so much easier for me than it has been in the past.

"What do you envision your life looking like in ten years?" She wiggles her eyebrows, clearly pleased with the question she thought of.

"That's a good one," I compliment. "Let's see. I obviously want to keep climbing the real estate ladder. I'd love to have a brokerage firm of my own someday. Maybe even expand and open another branch in another state. What about you?"

A look that I can only describe as peaceful joy comes over her face as she thinks. "I want it all," she says, voice barely above a whisper. "I want to keep the title of one of the top three realtors on the island. I want the marriage. The babies. The house of my own. The beach picnics. The family luaus. The adventures. I want it all."

My chest tightens as I imagine what a life like that would look like. To make more time for things outside of work. It doesn't seem half-bad. In fact, it sounds pretty darn amazing the more I think about it. I nod and smile at her response. "Sounds like an awesome life."

The ringing of my phone interrupts us. But instead of answering, I silence it and slide it back in my pocket, feeling only a slight urge to answer it.

"You can answer that," Tori says.

"No, it's okay. I don't want to be rude. And I'm learning how to focus on other things."

"Really, it's okay," she says, lifting her brows to assure me. "I promise. I understand more than anyone. I'll never ask you to completely cut work out. I know it means a lot to you. Go for it, honestly."

"Are you sure?" I ask warily, slowly reaching for my still-ringing phone.

"Yes," she insists. I decide to go with it and answer on the very last ring, but I don't feel the need to move away from Tori. I stay glued to her side as I make the phone call as quick as I possibly can.

"That was Rudy," I tell her once I hang up, "calling with his RSVP to the gala. He'll be bringing a potential buyer with him."

"Great! Ah, I can't believe the gala is in just a few days," Tori breathes, looking out at the ocean. "There's so much work to do before then."

"Hey, we aren't supposed to be talking about work, remember?" I nudge her with my elbow.

"Oh, yeah," she says sheepishly.

I push myself off the sand and twist back to her. "How about dessert?"

She looks up at me, a loose line of still-damp hair drifting across her face from the wind. As she tucks it back behind her ear, I hold eye contact and reach out my hand.

"Dinner and dessert. How lucky am I?" When she stands, she hooks her hand in the crook of my elbow.

"You need to raise your standards if being fed is anything other than a given," I say, tossing our trash into a nearby can and then leading us across the sand. It's still plenty warm, but there's a slight chill to the air as the sun slowly starts to descend over the horizon.

"I have a terrible track record when it comes to dating." She smirks, squeezing a little bit closer to my side as we walk along the uneven sand. "I'd say my standards are pretty low at this point—which, hey, is good news for you!"

"I'll take it. Anything to help my chances. We both know my game isn't top-notch."

Her giggle in response brings a smile to my lips, despite the obvious dig.

"For the record," I say quietly, growing serious, wanting to get my words right. "Anyone who didn't see what an absolute catch you are is a fool."

She looks down at the sand, her hair falling to cover the beginning of her smile.

"Thank you," she says, lifting her gaze back to mine. "You're a catch too."

"I feel like you're obligated to say that now, but I'll take it anyway. Shave ice or smoothie bowl?" I ask, pointing to two nearby food trucks.

"Shave ice, please."

We walk in silence, the sound of waves crashing onto shore and the noise from fellow beach-goers the only sound in the air.

Luckily, there's no line, and we're able to order our cups quickly —blue raspberry and lilikoi flavor for her, cherry and lemonade for me.

We walk through the cluster of picnic tables and find one that's on the outer edge and the most secluded. Climbing to sit on top, we rest our feet on the bench seat and angle toward where the sun is now starting to disappear over the ocean. We scoop out our shave ice and eat in a comfortable silence, people-watching and watching the horizon.

Even though there's only about three inches or so of space between us, that suddenly feels like way too much. So as I scrape the bottom of my shave ice bowl, I set it down on my left and then attempt to stretch out my right arm, bringing it around Tori's back. At the last moment, I hesitate, deciding between resting my hand on her waist or over her shoulder.

I go with placing my hand on her waist, gently resting it against her dress. Out of the corner of my eye, I can see her push her lips together in an attempt to stop a smile.

"Is this you flirting?" she asks playfully.

"That depends," I say, my voice unintentionally coming out low. "Is it working?"

When she turns her head to me, the energy between us seems to affect her too, and any sign of playfulness is gone from her expression. She rolls her lips before shrugging.

"It's not...*NOT* working," she says in a whisper, her eyes connecting with mine.

Once again, the buzz I feel when we're together gives me a surge of confidence, and I capitalize on that by moving in for a kiss. It's gentle and quick. But it causes feelings to stir inside of me that I realize I'm starting to become addicted to. I'm not sure what this means for us and for our future, but I know without a doubt that this is something I want to explore. I smile and squeeze her closer to my side, inhaling a breath of her hair as I do.

And we sit there, squished together, as we watch the remainder of the sunset. It's not at all how I envisioned we'd be watching the sunset tonight, but somehow, it's turned out even better.

21

TORI

"Exactly," I say into my phone as I walk through the doors of my condo building. "Take the night to think it over, and then just let me know in the morning if you'd like to submit an offer. Then I can meet you at any time to go over paperwork if needed."

"Perfect. Thank you, Tori," Sharon, my client who's considering purchasing one of my quaint beachside bungalow listings, says on the other line.

"Of course. Call me with any questions. Take your time, but remember that house won't sit on the market for very long," I tell her before we say goodbye and disconnect the phone call.

Grabbing my key out of my purse, I open my mailbox and, once again, find a tiny piece of paper directing me to the main office.

"Hi, Jenny," I say, knocking on the already open door of the office on the other side of the entryway, which I've visited quite a bit these past few days.

"Ah, Tori. Nice to see you again. I think we've interacted more in this last week than we have the entire time you've been living here, don't you think?" She smiles at me warmly.

"I think you're right," I laugh, trading the slip of paper for the stack of mail that was too large to fit in my tiny mailbox.

"We might be best friends by the new year if you keep getting this many cards," she points out.

"It's looking that way. Thanks, Jenny! I'm sure I'll see you again tomorrow." I tuck the mail under my arm and head toward the elevators.

"Good evening," I say to the woman from the ninth floor, who I've recently discovered is named Rachel, as she passes by me in the direction of the front doors.

"Have a great night." She smiles back at me.

When I make it all the way up and inside my condo, I drop everything on the kitchen island, slip my strappy sandals off, and shred the lightweight blazer that, although it did keep me a touch too warm, I absolutely needed to wear today as it matches perfectly with my cream skirt. A text message comes through just as I wrap the blazer around the back of a stool. When I grab my phone, I see a new message in the group chat with my sisters.

Emily: I still think it's rude that Tori hasn't given us any details of her date last night.

I roll my eyes and huff a laugh at the same time. It's not that I'm avoiding my sisters, but I've been too busy to fill them in yet. And also, there's a part of me that likes the idea of keeping the details between Connor and me. I don't need their opinions to know that it was amazing, and I've been over-the-moon giddy about it all day. Another message comes through before I can even set my phone down.

Grace: Super rude. How are we ever supposed to find out if they're a match made in heaven?

Emily: Or if there was a kiss?

Ava: Maybe the kiss was bad, and that's why Tori hasn't mentioned it.

Tori: Tori is right here. Kiss(es) were amazing. I will not be answering any further questions. Emily, tell us about the wedding venue tour you went on today.

I turn my phone face down on the island and turn my focus to the mail.

"All right, let's get these opened," I mumble to myself, knowing that if I don't take care of these cards right away, they'll just pile up on the counter. I rip open the first one—a card with a couple that appears to be on a Segway tour in Philadelphia, Pennsylvania. I smile at their cheesy grins and bring it over to the wall near the front door where I've hung several copper string lights. After clipping the card on with an empty clip, I grab the battery pack at the bottom and turn the lights on, causing each of the clips to light up and give off a warm white glow.

The next card is a family from Charleston, South Carolina, with cute twin girls in the forefront. *Happy Holidays from the Conrad's—Jared, Laura, Taylor, and Lennon.* I go through each card—seven in total today—and clip them onto the string light display. I might need to get another set soon if I keep getting this many every day. Not that I know any of these people, but it's worth hanging them solely for the look on Elliot's face when I FaceTimed him this morning to show him.

The next several cards get opened—ones from Edmond, Oklahoma; Ladera Ranch, California; and Menomonee Falls, Wisconsin—when several text message notifications come through at the same time. Expecting to see several from my sisters, I smile when one also comes through from Connor.

Connor: How was your day?

Goosebumps spark across my skin at the mere sight of his name. I haven't seen him all day. Both of us were busy with other projects, so we've been texting off and on all day long instead. Before answering back right away, I hurry through sorting the rest of the mail. Then I make myself a quick turkey-and-provolone sandwich and grab a handful of crackers to throw on the plate. I take that, plus a glass of wine, to the balcony. Leaving the sliding door open, I grab a blanket, settle onto a lounge chair, and reach for my phone. Ignoring the group text with my sisters for now—that already has eleven unread messages—I open the one from Connor.

Tori: Super productive! Just sat down on the balcony to relax. You?

Connor: Just got home. Maybe I'll do the same.

Tori: You don't have a balcony.

Tori: And barely a couch to relax on.

Connor: Touché. Hold tight.

I grab for a cracker and munch on it, peering at the empty pool below, the twinkling lights from the palm trees above the pool reflecting across the top of the water. Someone from a floor or two below me is playing Christmas music from inside their condo, and the faint sound drifts up to me. It doesn't take long before my phone buzzes again.

Connor: I'm all set.

The next message is an image of him sitting on his couch, his legs stretched out in front of him, feet resting on the floor where a coffee table should be.

Tori: Looks comfy.

Connor: Truthfully, I can't remember the last time I sat on the couch without my laptop. It feels weird. Like I should be doing something.

Tori: You are doing something. You're relaxing.

Connor: Not sure if I like it.

Tori: It takes some getting used to. You're doing great!

Tori: What are you going to do now? Watch a movie? Read a book?

Connor: I think I'll just sit here and talk to you for a while, if you don't mind?

A blush heats my cheeks, and it's really a shame how much his words affect me.

Tori: I don't mind. Although, you will see me in just seven short hours at the office.

Connor: That won't be nearly enough. Have dinner with me tomorrow night. At my place?

Butterflies swarm in my stomach, and I pull the blanket up and over my mouth, only partially covering my grin. I've always known Connor to be straightforward and intense, but only in the workplace. Seeing these little glimpses of him being bossy and blunt when it comes to this new dating situation that we're feeling out…it's exhilarating.

> Tori: I can squeeze you in.

> Connor: I have a showing at five, so I'll pick you up on my way home.

> Tori: Perfect!

> Connor: Okay…I tried. I can't sit here any longer. I'm going to do a quick workout and then answer some emails before bed.

> Tori: You lasted longer than I thought you would! Good effort!

> Connor: See you in the morning?

> Tori: See you in the morning. Goodnight, Connor.

> Connor: Goodnight, Tori.

I set my phone down on my stomach and slide even lower until I'm in a half-lying position. Taking a deep breath, I take a bite of my sandwich and realize that I can't remember the last time I felt this content and happy.

22

CONNOR

"Oh, I love when the blueberries cover most of the pancake," Tori says over my shoulder in my kitchen, peering down at the cast-iron pan on the stovetop.

"Doesn't it make it all mushy?" I ask, cringing at the goopy mess of purple-twinged batter.

"Yes. That's what's so great about it." Tori lifts herself up onto the counter next to me before grabbing a spatula.

"I'm more of a three-blueberries-max-per-pancake kind of guy," I say as she leans over slightly to flip the pancakes, the vanilla scent of her perfume mixing with the nutty aroma of the pancakes, creating a deliciously warm and somehow comforting scent.

"Minimalistic, even with your pancakes," she teases with a smile. She uses the spatula to scoop each pancake onto the plate that I hold out for her. Then she takes the cold stick of butter and runs it along the pan, leaving a sizzling wake of melting butter as she goes. When it's fully greased, I spoon some batter, repeating until there are four even circles starting to brown. Over the last half-hour, we've developed a nice pancake-making system, Tori and I.

"Here, you can do the honors," I say, handing her the bowl of blueberries. She starts dropping them onto the batter in rapid succession, but she only drops three blueberries onto two of them.

"Oh!" She hops off the counter after her gaze spans across the room. "I can't believe we forgot to turn the tree on!" She crosses the living room, past the couch that is newly adorned with a blanket lying across the back and two giant throw pillows that Tori brought over tonight. I don't even mind that she's making minor changes like that at my house. In fact, if anything, it makes me happy. I want this to be a place that she feels comfortable being at.

"I still don't have any ornaments," I say across the room as she crouches down behind the tree.

"I see that. At least you have lights." She plugs in the lights, illuminating the tree in a white glow, before coming back to the kitchen, where her phone buzzes for the third time. She lets out an exasperated sigh.

"Ugh, sorry," she says, hopping back on the counter before tapping away on her phone. "If I don't answer my sisters, they'll never stop. I just need to tell them which dress I decided to wear tonight."

"And that's necessary information for them?" I ask, flipping the pancakes.

"It's a whole thing. We always send each other pictures of what we're planning to wear on dates. For the record, they thought you would prefer my yellow dress instead of this blue one."

I give her a blank stare, not sure what the best response is supposed to be. She looks absolutely gorgeous in blue, but yellow is one of my favorite colors. Did they know that? And am I supposed to side with the sisters when it comes to stuff like this?

"This feels like a trap," I say slowly.

She bursts into a laugh, dropping her head and letting her hair fall into her face. When she brings it back up, she reaches out and squeezes my arm.

"That is definitely not something you need to stress about. Trust me. Let me handle my sisters."

"If you say so," I say with a hesitant smile, lifting the plate for her to slide the fresh pancakes on. I turn the burners on the stove off and grab the bowl of fruit salad and a carton of syrup out of the fridge. I follow Tori, who's carrying the pancakes, to my kitchen table.

"There," I say, pointing to the food with a proud smile. "Breakfast for dinner."

"I love it." Her tone has me lifting my eyes across the table to hers, where she hits me with the sweetest smile. Returning the smile, I hold her gaze, getting sucked into her ocean-blue eyes momentarily while I pass her a plate.

This seems to keep happening more and more often. What's meant to be a quick glance ends up being a full-on moment that we get sucked into, getting stuck in each other's gazes longer than intended. Not that I'm complaining. Something about the connection always ends up putting me at ease.

"So I wonder how Beth's showing at Makana Manor is going tonight," I say, scooping a spoonful of fruit onto my plate.

"Hopefully, terrible. Is that bad to say?" She pauses and cringes. "That was awful."

"Terrible. But I hope so too."

"Anyway, I'm excited to decorate tomorrow," she says before popping a pancake bite into her mouth. "I'll run and grab the garland and stockings if you want to swing by and grab some more lights? Then we can meet at Makana to get everything set up?"

"I can handle that."

"Then nobody else at work should be going by the house tomorrow night, right? It's still blocked off on the calendar in the break room? I forgot to double-check and make sure nobody messed with it," she says.

"Yeah, I looked at it before I left the office today. Makana is all ours tomorrow and the next day for the gala. I believe Beth has another showing scheduled for the day after, but we should be all cleaned out by then," I say, piercing a strawberry slice with my fork.

"Perfect." She grabs another pancake off the pile and pours syrup over the top of it before happily digging in. We finish eating, and as we clear the table, a twinge of insecurity suddenly forms in my stomach, unsure of what we should do next. I didn't plan anything out beyond dinner, and it's been ages since I've had a woman over to my place—or really, ever. She gives me a sidelong glance and must sense the change in my demeanor.

"Let's leave the dishes for later," she suggests. "Want to come sit by the pool with me?"

The gentle yet almost daring look in her eyes makes the bubbling nerves melt away, completely putting me at ease with just one look.

"I'd like that," I say quietly. Taking her hand in mine, I lead her out the sliding doors, where a slightly brisk gust of wind immediately rushes over us with the evening air.

"I love this time of year," Tori says, hiking up her blue dress and bending down to sit on the ledge of the pool, sliding her feet in the water.

"Christmastime?" I ask, lowering myself next to her.

"Yeah, I love everything about the holiday season," she says dreamily. "The way everything is decorated with lights. The cooler, more bearable weather. The yummy, festive food. Santa walking around in surf shorts. All of it."

I chuckle. "What does Christmas Day look like for you?" The bright-pink polish on her toes is distracting as she lazily moves her feet around in the water.

"Well, it's loud and crazy, as you can imagine. But it's also magical, especially watching my nieces and nephew. We all gather at my parents' house in the morning and pretty much spend the entire day there. What about you?" She grips the edge of the pool with both hands, straightening her arms and shifting forward a little bit before looking over her shoulder at me.

"It's usually pretty quiet, actually." I shrug, trying not to get distracted by the way her dress is bunching up around her waist, revealing a little bit more of the skin on her thighs with each movement she makes.

"Surely you don't work on Christmas Day," she says pointedly, raising her brows.

"I don't do much, but not by choice. It's not that I don't want to work. It's that nobody else does," I admit with a smirk. "I learned early on that no one is going to answer my emails or phone calls on that day. But I do usually end up catching up on emails and forms and such. My parents come over to spend the day with my grandparents, so I usually make it over there at some point." I shrug.

"Sounds nice," she says sincerely and in a way that I don't feel judged at all that I basically just admitted I would rather work than celebrate Christmas. We sit in a comfortable silence for a while, kicking our feet in the water, and it only crosses my mind once that I left my phone in the house.

"This is nice." I smile at her, tapping her arm with my elbow. "Thanks for coming over tonight."

"Thanks for inviting me," she says, the corner of her mouth lifting up into a smirk. Her eyes linger on mine, and I lean in slowly to bring my lips to hers. Her mouth presses back against mine in a firm yet gentle way. I bring my hand to rest on her jawline, my fingertips sliding through her thick hair. Goosebumps spark across the top of my skin, and my heartbeat picks up speed with each second that we're locked in the kiss.

When we separate, she scoots closer to me, wrapping her arms around my arm and resting her head on my shoulder. And we enjoy a quiet night by the pool, positioned just like that, enjoying each other's easy company. I feel a contentment that is new to me the entire time, even when a cloud of anticipation eventually forms in the air of all the activity and pressure of what the next couple of days will bring.

23

TORI

"It's a little crooked." I hear Connor's voice from behind me as I adjust the massive red orchid-adorned wreath, attempting to get it perfectly centered against the front door at Makana Manor.

"Really?" I reply, frowning at the wreath, taking a few steps back to examine it. Connor reaches the top step and comes to a stop by my side.

"No," he says swiftly, placing a kiss on my temple. "It looks perfect."

He lets out a huff when I slap him across the chest.

"Not funny. I'm stressed out," I admit, feeling overwhelmed and a bit flustered.

"Hey, don't be stressed," he says, concern etched in his voice as he wraps his arm around the top of my shoulder. "It's going to be great."

I take a deep breath, trying to relax into his embrace, but the extensive to-do list that's running through my mind is making it hard to do. I notice what he's wearing and try to be discreet in appreciating how good he looks in black basketball shorts and a white T-shirt. I think I should try and get him to dress casually more often.

"Okay." I clap my hands together, feeling anxious to continue on. "Back to work. Did you grab the lights?"

"I did," he says, holding the bag up. "These are going inside, right? On the staircase?"

"Yes. And then the lighting company will be here within the hour to start hanging lights along the exterior roof and up these columns too." I separate from Connor to pat one of the large concrete beams.

"Awesome. I'll head in and start on the staircase."

"The party rental company is already inside setting up, too," I call before he reaches the front door.

"Stay out of their way—got it." He clutches the front door handle and throws me a confident smile. "See you in a bit."

When he closes the front door behind him, I refocus on the wreath, determining that it is, in fact, centered. I shift my focus to the left side of the front porch, where I lay an ivory tablecloth over a rectangular table and start assembling our homemade wreath party favors onto it. With each wreath I lay against each other, I mentally run through the names of the realtors and guests on the list for tomorrow's event. We have over three hundred RSVPs, including agents, potential buyers, and of course, some family and friends who are mainly coming to show support. Although, I think my family really just wants to see the property in person after seeing all the pictures I've shared. But that's more than okay. The more guests there are, the more appeal it brings.

When I get the wreaths arranged as best I can, I skip down the stairs and open the back of Matt's truck that I borrowed again and check to make sure the flowers all survived the drive over here. Twenty small pots of white and red poinsettias are tucked together closely inside of the truck bed. Grabbing one in each hand, I arrange one pot along the right side of the sprawling staircase, then one on each step. Sweat starts forming along my hairline as I work, the humidity starting to get to me, but I brush it away and start doing the same to the left side.

Feeling grateful for going with my own casual attire today and opting for my biker shorts and an oversized tee, I run my sweaty palms along my shorts and step back to make sure all of the flowers are arranged evenly along the stairs. Catching my breath, I take a few sips of my water bottle and nod, pleased with the way they look, and shut the trunk.

Skipping two steps at a time, I push open the front door, where I'm greeted by a very welcome blast of air conditioning. I notice that Mariah Carey's "All I Want for Christmas is You" is playing loudly on the surround sound system. Stifling a laugh, I shut the door behind me.

"I'm guessing this was not your song choice," I say to Connor, who's pushing his lips together in aggravation from where he's standing halfway up the staircase. In one hand, he holds a jumble of lights, and the other is guiding the string around the staircase banister.

"I put the local radio station on," he grumbles quietly, untying some lights that had gotten tangled. "But then I told Cindy over there that she could choose a song since she's been working so long setting up the tables in silence." He pauses and looks pointedly at me. "That was four songs ago, Tori. I don't know how much more I can take."

"I'll pick the next song," I assure him with a smile. "I'll be in the living room if you need me."

"Lights are looking great, by the way!" I call out, already walking away from the stairs. "Oh, these are stunning," I gasp, stopping to admire the high-top tables that the crew is setting up all along this main walkway area.

"Thanks, Tori," Cindy from the party rental company says. "Oh, and I need to know what you'd like to do here. What do you think about adding another table or two right in this space?" She points to the empty area next to her.

"Hmm." I touch my chin as I think. "Actually, let's not. I'd like to keep this entryway and the area by the tree as open as possible for any dancing. Plus, the band will be set up in this area over here, so we don't want it to be too crowded."

"Okay," she agrees with an amenable smile, continuing to tie the ivory cloth that's draping over the high-top into a bow against the leg of the table.

"Thank you. Let me know if you have any other questions. I'll be right over here." I head past the kitchen, making a quick pit stop at the audio system on the wall to change the music to a soft Christmas variety and move on to the living room, where I set my bags on the coffee table. I scan the fireplace, envisioning what I have in mind, then get to work pulling things out of the bags. I start with wrapping the garland atop the mantel, weaving it around the tall candlesticks, and re-arranging everything a few times to get it just right before hanging a few gold-speckled white stockings on either side of the mantel. Lastly, I string a gold *Mele Kalikimaka* sign in between the stockings, completing the cozy fireplace decor.

The next couple of hours pass by in a blur. I get lost in the music and zero in on each specific task at hand while also fielding calls and emails from people sending in last-minute RSVPs. After the mantel is finished, I set up a small white-lit tree in the corner of the living room and throw an ivory plush blanket over the back of the couch to add a little extra coziness to this luxury coastal beach house. Connor and I make a trip to our cars to haul another load of bags in, and then we head upstairs, decorating that level well into the late evening.

"What do you think?" I ask him, hands on my hips, admiring the primary bedroom that we just finished. The fireplace is decorated similarly to the one downstairs, and each nightstand has white snowflakes and added greenery atop them. There are two white wire reindeer figures in the corner.

"I think it looks magical," he replies, his tone making me smile. I know the amount of effort we just put into getting this place gala ready was not something that he thoroughly enjoyed, but I also know that he agrees that it was necessary to make tomorrow the best it can possibly be. We walk down the hallway, past the bedrooms, each one complete with their own tree and a sprinkle of decorations.

"You don't even need to praise me on this staircase. I already know it's the best-wrapped one you've ever seen," he says as we make our way down the stairs. With the rental company people long gone, the rest of the house is quiet except for the soft music.

"You did such a good job. I had no idea you were so handy at wrapping a string around a pole," I tease.

"Hey, that took major coordination and technique." He slides an arm around my waist as we walk past the grand tree and the high-top tables, admiring the final look. We pause near the kitchen island, where his fingers flex against my hip, the warmth of his touch traveling all the way up to my chest. Leaning into his touch, I slide my arm around his waist, resting my hand on the rim of his basketball shorts, and bring my other arm around his front to clasp with my hand, resting them on his hip bone. After a few moments of silence, quietly taking everything in, I take a deep breath.

"It's going to be great, right?" I whisper, feeling anticipation fluttering in my stomach. He squeezes me closer to his side.

"It's going to be great."

24

———

CONNOR

"This looks absolutely incredible," Tori says breathily from the same spot in the kitchen that we were standing in last night.

"Unbelievably stunning," I agree in a low voice. But unlike her, I'm not talking about the way that the house is literally sparkling. Everything is in its place and perfectly pristine. Ready and waiting in anticipation for guests to arrive. I'm talking about the way that she looks in her olive-green floor-length satin dress. Her wild hair is tamed in big, wavy curls that are pulled back on one side with a gold clip, and the way her dress is open in the back is making it difficult for me to breathe normally. She's so incredibly beautiful that it almost hurts, and I was rendered completely speechless when I picked her up earlier. Focusing on the road and not on her proved to be a challenge on the drive over, but I managed to keep my eyes and my hands to myself long enough to get us here.

"Dance with me," I blurt out, making her snap her head toward me.

"What?" she laughs while I extend my hand, acting on the sudden urge to be as close as I possibly can to her.

"Now? We have to—"

"Everything's done," I assure her, leading her across the entryway, her heels clanking against the tile floor. We walk past the three-person band that's just starting to set up along the far wall, and we come to a stop by the large Christmas tree.

"But the guests will be here soon," she says in a feeble attempt to protest, but her will must not be strong because she readily steps closer into my arms.

"Just dance with me," I insist. My eyes lock with hers as she presses herself lightly against my chest. I hold her hand in mine against the jacket of my black tux as my other hand comes to rest on her lower back, my fingertips lightly brushing against the bare skin of her open back. Simultaneously, her other arm slides behind my neck, curling her fingers against my collar.

The flash of heat that pulses behind her eyes at my touch sends a quiet buzz of electricity all the way across my skin. The hint of a blush colors her cheeks, along with a shy smile, when two guys from the band start playing a slow song just for us.

"You," I say quietly against her temple, "are breathtaking tonight."

She tightens her fingertips against my neck in response before craning her neck to look up at me and smirk. "Look at you, being all smooth and charming." Her smile softens. "What happened to being nervous around women?"

"Not with you," I answer honestly. "And not when you look like that."

She leans her head forward, closing her eyes as we sway slowly back and forth. I dip my head, relishing in the energy that's sparking between us. In the past, this would have absolutely made me flustered. I would have been way out of my league. But once again, it feels different with her.

Everything is different.

Ignoring the occasional glances from the wait staff that's bustling in the background, we stay lost in our own little world and soak up these few minutes of quiet before we'll inevitably need to shift into work mode. When she lifts her head and pulls back slightly, I take that as a sign and run my fingers gently up her bare spine.

"Thank you for the dance," I say, once again getting pulled into her stare. A tiny part of me wants to stay on the dance floor, with her in my arms, for the entire evening. But the bigger, more responsible part of me wins out, knowing what's at stake tonight, and we separate. But not before I grab her hand to keep her close as we walk.

"Thank you," she replies with a side smile. "I think I needed that."

I throw a wink to the band as a silent thank-you as we walk to the kitchen, where I reluctantly squeeze her hand one last time before dropping it and attempting to clear my mind.

"Okay." She wiggles her fingers, seemingly also attempting to shake off whatever just transpired between us. She looks around, and I watch as she blows out a slow breath.

"The food is ready. All the trees are lit. Booklets are ready." She taps the top of the hardcover books we had made that give you an in-depth idea of what it would be like to live here— including all amenities, nearby attractions, and even a section that has suggestions for hosting other events at various other times of the year.

"We're as good as we're going to get." The words are barely out of my mouth when the front door opens and our first guests come inside. Tori throws me a quick, exhilarated smile, and we walk side by side to greet them. Determination surges through me as I shift completely into professional mode, laser-focusing on the job ahead of us tonight.

"Roger." I shake hands with the fellow agent I recognize from Maui, who's looking dapper in his dark-gray tux.

"Connor, nice to see you." He returns the handshake and gestures toward the brunette woman in a long silver dress that's by his side. "This is my wife, Rita. She so graciously agreed to come with me tonight."

"He had to pull my arm, but I finally agreed," she teases. "This place is beautiful."

"Glad you could both make it. Come on in." I gesture for them to come in with my hand, pointing to the area next to the door.

"I'd love it if you could show us around. I have a few clients in mind for this property. I promised one in New York that I'd FaceTime them at some point tonight and show them around," Roger says.

"Absolutely," I say. "Let's head this way." I throw one last glance at Tori, who's greeting the second group of people to arrive, before leading Roger and Rita down the hall. We all grab a glass of champagne from the waiter carrying a tray nearby.

"So let's start in this section of the house," I say once we enter the kitchen area. "In here, we have a chef's kitchen equipped with high-end appliances, and there is plenty of storage and counter space. There's a beverage fridge down here and even a warming drawer to keep food warm before serving."

"Is this marble?" Rita asks, running her hand along the island countertop.

"It is." I nod before opening the pantry door. "And we have a climate-controlled pantry with a microwave and its own sink."

"Very nice quality," Roger says, opening a cabinet drawer.

"Off to the right here, we have the dining area, with plenty of seating as you can see, and then the living area, which might be my personal favorite space in the house." I lay a hand on the back of the sofa and watch them admire the grand fireplace that's perfectly decorated and festive. I'm hoping it's easy for everyone to imagine this as being the perfect place to snuggle up and enjoy the holidays with your loved ones. Judging by the looks on their faces, I'm thinking they might agree.

"Back here, we have the laundry and a half bath." I lead them through the spacious laundry room that is, of course, decorated with Christmas signs and small artificial trees on the countertop.

I retrace our steps and take them back through the living room and out the open sliding doors to the outdoor space. A mugginess hangs in the air as I let them roam, taking it all in. There are high-tops set up around the perimeter of the pool and twinkling lights hanging off the exterior roof of the house.

"Stunning," Roger says, nodding his head in approval. "I can't wait to show my clients."

I lead them back inside, show them the elevator, and then we head up the back staircase. I guide them through each bedroom, bathroom, and closet. After showing them the entire layout upstairs, we promise to keep in touch within the next couple of days and exchange handshakes. I leave them to FaceTime his clients, take a deep breath, and head back downstairs to greet the next group.

25

———

TORI

"Yes, obviously cash offers are more appealing in general," I tell Sarah, who did, in fact, make it all the way back in town for the gala with her husband, Micah, in tow. "But I do believe this seller is more interested in it being a full-ask offer versus what the logistics of it are. He's turned down some pretty solid offers in the past just because it wasn't at full asking. So that's something to keep in mind."

"Okay, that's good to know," Sarah says with a nod, looking deep in thought. I lean a hip against the counter in the upstairs bathroom, where we stopped to chat and allow myself to feel a tiny spark of excitement that, just maybe, Connor and I might be able to bring a buyer to our boss and win this competition. The thought that we might be potentially close to winning causes adrenaline to rush through my veins.

"What do you think, Micah?" Sarah asks her husband, who's

slowly pacing the perimeter of the bathroom, inspecting every little detail.

"I really like it," he says, running his hand along his jawline. "We have some things to discuss privately, but I don't see why this wouldn't be a top contender for sure."

"I agree," Sarah replies.

"Do you guys have any more questions for me?" I ask.

"Not that I can think of off the top of my head, but I'm sure I'll think of some. Oh, I'd love to see the kitchen one more time," Sarah says.

"Absolutely. Let's head back down." I start leading them out of the bathroom. "I'm so glad you guys were able to make it—"

I'm interrupted when we practically run right into Rich as we turn the corner into the bedroom.

"Pardon me," he says, looking a little bit like he was just caught with his hand in the cookie jar.

"Rich," I say in greeting, trying my best to be warm and welcoming, despite my instant annoyance. "This is Sarah and Micah. They came all the way from Utah to be here tonight."

"Pleasure to meet you," he says with a crooked grin, looking somewhat uncomfortable as he slides his hands into his tux pockets. I wonder what he's up to and why he's roaming around, lurking in the hallways by himself.

"Rich is a fellow agent at my firm," I explain as they shake hands.

"We were just on our way back downstairs." I wave as we skirt around him, not wanting to expose them to one of Rich's long-winded stories. Luckily, Sarah and Micah follow closely behind me, and we head back down the stairs.

"Feel free to roam around the kitchen and enjoy the gala," I tell them as we reach the main level, the music from the band now loud enough that I need to raise my voice. "Get comfortable and really try to envision yourselves here. Let me know if you have any questions, but otherwise, I'll leave you two to soak it all in."

"Thank you, Tori," Sarah says with a genuine hug.

"I'll touch base within the next few days," I say. When they saunter off, a hand grips my elbow, spinning me around until I'm face-to-face with my friend Quinn.

"Eek!" We both try to dial our shrieks down into respectable muffled squeals as we hug.

"Ah, I haven't seen you in, like, a month!" I say, pulling back to look her over.

"I know! It's so good to be back. I'm realizing that a month is way too long to be away from home," she says, happiness practically exuding off of her.

"You went right from Bali to the Maldives, right? Were you able to finish your assignment there?" I scoot us a little bit off to the side so we can have some privacy away from the other gala guests.

"I did. I got fresh images of the resort and its amenities so they can update their website."

"That's great, Quinn," I say.

"Yeah! They're happy with the final images, and it was a breathtaking trip, but nothing beats home, you know? Enough about that, though. How are you? This gala is amazing. You totally nailed it."

"Thank you." I beam. "It's a great turnout, isn't it?"

"It's amazing," she says sincerely, looking around the room before snapping her head back to face me. "Okay, who's that gorgeous specimen of a man that keeps looking at you?"

"Who?" I ask innocently, although I don't know why I bother asking, and I surely don't look around to see who she's referencing. I already know she's talking about Connor. We've been stealing glances all night—little nods and winks whenever the opportunity arises. Like right now, I glance his way, and he gives me a curt dip of his head, looking dashingly handsome in his tux. His dark hair and tanned skin make him look incredibly sexy in his black formalwear. Powerful and sophisticated. Intense and commanding. Such a blatant disparity to the fumbling, awkward man that I've sometimes seen. Admittedly, I'm realizing that I like any and all versions of him.

"Um, the person you're staring back at," she laughs.

"Connor," I say simply, as if his name is all the explanation I need to give.

"Connor," she repeats. "Work Connor?"

"Yup." I pull my gaze away from him and blush at Quinn. "He's a little more than just Work Connor now."

"I can see that." An amused smile tugs at the corner of her mouth.

My gaze flicks behind her shoulder at an agent who just walked in the front door, a couple following closely behind.

"Listen, obviously, we need to catch up, but I need to keep moving," I say with an apologetic cringe.

"Oh, absolutely. Go kick some real-estate butt. You got this." She winks and gives me a hug before crossing the room to join her fiancé, Brian; her brother, John; and his very pregnant wife, Mia, who are all gathered around a high-top table. I make a mental note to catch up with all of them later and manage a quick wave to Matt and Paige, who are on their way to join their group.

Just as I'm about to turn and greet the agent, I catch sight of my sisters huddled closely together near the kitchen. It takes me a second to register who they're huddled around, but once it does, I mumble under my breath, panic shooting down my core.

"Agh, shoot." I quickly glance in the other direction and see that the agent has already disappeared into the sea of people, so I rush across the room to where my sisters are standing with Connor's mom and dad. Connor had pointed them out in passing when I was talking to Grace earlier, and I should have known that they would be waiting to pounce on them as soon as they could.

"Mr. And Mrs. Brooks," I say politely, everyone turning in my direction as I approach. "I'm Tori. It's so nice to meet you." I shake their hands as they smile broadly at me.

"Oh, please, call me Kathy," his mom says warmly. The twinkle in her eye tells me that Connor has mentioned who I am. Relief washes over me that there isn't an ounce of scrutiny or disapproval in her expression.

"I see you've met my sisters." I make eye contact with Emily, who smiles sweetly with a twinge of guilt in her eyes. I silently hope that they haven't said anything too embarrassing about me.

"We have. They were just telling us all about you and your family. I'm surprised that we haven't crossed paths before."

"It was bound to happen at some point, I'm sure," I say.

"Beautiful party," his dad mentions, scanning the room.

"Tori and Connor have worked really hard on this," Ava chimes in before I can reply.

"She's as hard-working as she is stunning," Grace says, and I inwardly cringe.

"Thank you," I say, gesturing toward all three sisters. "Oh hey, Matt asked me to send you guys his way. He has a question for all of us siblings, I guess." I don't even feel slightly bad that I just threw Matt under the bus. I'd rather him deal with my sisters than Connor's parents, especially when they haven't had a chance to warm up to them.

"We're going to keep mingling anyway," Kathy says. "It was a pleasure meeting you all, especially you, Tori."

"The pleasure's all mine." I smile as they walk off, then out of the corner of my eye, I see another agent walk through the front door.

"I'll meet you guys over there," I tell my sisters, shooing them in the direction of Matt before walking toward the door.

"Jim, thank you for coming." I reach my hand out for a handshake as several people come all the way inside.

"Wow, Tori. This listing is incredible. Thank you for having us," Jim says, shutting the door behind him. "These are my clients, Linda and Bill."

"Welcome. Please come in." I smile, waving them in. "Would you like me to show you around? Or would you prefer to grab something to eat first?"

"We'd love it if you could show us around, actually," Linda says. "We're anxious to see the place."

"Absolutely, my pleasure," I guide them through a few couples who are dancing near the band and stop when we cross paths with a waiter effortlessly carrying a full tray of drinks.

"Champagne?" I ask, waiting for all three of them to take a glass before continuing on with a tour of the kitchen and living area.

"This outdoor area is one of my favorite features of the whole property," I say, leading them onto the patio, where the string lights and pool give off a soft glow in the almost completely dark evening sky.

"Oh, this is a great size pool. Definitely more than enough room for when out-of-town guests are visiting," Linda says.

"Definitely," I agree. "You also have your own stretch of private beach. You'll have to come back in the daylight to see that. It's unreal."

A waitress passes by with spicy tuna crispy rice bite appetizers, which they all take without hesitation. I politely decline, as I've already had at least four, and I'm trying not to outrun my luck for not spilling any sauce on my dress yet.

"That was fantastic. Maybe we should get a quick bite to eat before heading upstairs," Jim suggests, to which Linda and Bill agree.

"Take your time, and just let me know if you have any questions about the house. I'll be around all night," I say. As they head back inside, I hang back, scanning the party slowly and taking it all in. Filled with excitement, anticipation, and a sense of pride, I head back inside when I spot another agent I haven't greeted yet.

26

CONNOR

"Mele Kalikimaka," the very last party rental staffer calls out from the driveway before climbing in and driving off in his utility van, disassembled party tables and linens in tow. With a tired wave, I have a seat on the top step next to Tori and loosen my tie.

"We did it," she says, straightening her legs, resting her bare feet on a lower step, the slit in her dress falling open against her tan thigh and her heels splayed out next to her.

"We did it," I repeat, feeling exhaustion hit in full force. The night is quiet, a stark contrast to the bustling energy that was the gala just an hour before. It's a little hard to believe that, after all the planning and prepping, it's now all of a sudden over with.

Although, the work is far from over. Much of that is just beginning as, tomorrow morning, we plan to start following up with agents and answering the many inevitable questions that will come our way.

"I think you could have upped your description of the hardware in the bathrooms a little more, but other than that, I'd say it was a successful evening," I tease quietly, to which she rolls her eyes.

"I'm too tired to think of a comeback," she says drearily before perking up marginally. "Hey, I think we might get a serious offer from Sarah and Micah, though."

"Yeah? That's awesome. Roger seemed pretty confident that he'd have a serious buyer as well. Maybe we'll get into a bidding war. Can you imagine if we end up with an over-ask offer? Brad wouldn't know what to do."

"I'd be happy with one solid offer at this point."

"Did you see all the people dancing?" I ask.

"Yes! I knew the band was a good idea. And look, we only have one wreath left," she points to the lone wreath that we set aside before taking down the display table it was on earlier.

"I'm pretty sure that's one of yours," I tease.

"Ha ha." She smiles before taking a deep breath in and out, then covering a yawn with her hand.

"Come on. Let me get you home," I say, standing and turning to offer her my hand. She slowly looks up at me, hitting me with a look that houses both exhaustion and a flash of something more intense, making my heart skip a beat. Grabbing my hand, she keeps her eyes locked on mine and lifts herself off the steps until her legs brush against my thighs. She's on the step higher than me, which brings us face to face.

I can't resist the urge to lean in and press a soft kiss to her lips, squeezing her hand that's still in mine. Her free hand comes to the top of my shoulder, fingers brushing against the collar of my tux. I bring my hand to her hip and squeeze once before breaking away. A buzz and hungry need starts to ramp up deep in my stomach, like it always does when I kiss her, but I'm starkly aware of where we are. And on the steps of someone else's mansion—that I'm trying to sell—is not where I would like to have a make-out session, regardless of how tempting Tori is right now.

"I'll get the lights down here if you get the ones upstairs," she whispers, a fire still burning in her eyes as well.

"Deal," I say gruffly. We head back inside Makana Manor and make our rounds to ensure that all the lights are off and everything is back in its place. The Christmas decorations will stay up for now, but at least it's showing ready again. After putting the key back in the lockbox, I take her hand and lead her to my car.

"Can you do me a favor?" I ask Tori once we're buckled in and heading out of the front gates.

"What's that?" She leans her head back against the headrest, tilting it to peer over at me.

"Can you tell your sisters that green is my new favorite color that you wear?" I flick my eyes to her. "For the next time they ask?"

"Olive green?" She smiles sleepily.

"If that's what that is, then yes." I take her hand in mine, resting our joined hands on the center console as I drive.

The rest of the ride to her condo building is quiet, both exhaustion and a lingering spark in the air keeping my mind racing.

"You don't have to walk me all the way up, you know," she says when I park in her lot and start walking with her inside.

"Tori, it's past midnight. A gentleman walks you to your door," I say simply.

"I like when you're gentlemanly." She gives me a smile that I'm sure she means to be sweet, but it has a teasing twinge to it, which sends a swooping sensation low in my stomach.

We make it all the way to her floor, each step coated with a buzzing energy that has us walking as close to each other as possible. I'm not sure if it's the high from the gala or just the inevitable progression of feelings, but this feeling in my chest is borderline overwhelming. When we reach her door, I come behind her as she uses her keys, nuzzling my chin into her hair. The scent of her perfume is intoxicating, and I can't help but lay a hand on her hip, the silky smooth texture of her dress slipping against my fingers.

She leans her head to the side, allowing me to bring my head to her neck and my body closer to hers. Her shoulder rises and falls against where my mouth is hovering at the base of her neck as she takes a deep breath in and lets it all the way out—a telltale sign that she's as affected as I am right now.

She slowly turns, wedged between me and the door, until we're now facing each other, and she looks up at me. I can barely register the look in her eyes before she throws her arms around my neck and presses her mouth to mine. I waste no time and immediately grip both sides of her waist and slide my hands around to her lower back and hips. She scratches lightly at the base of my neck while I press her gently against the door, squeezing her hips at the same time.

I break the kiss and move to her jawline, fueled by the way that I feel when I'm with her this way. Confident. Bold. Powerful. She lifts her leg with the open slit and wraps it around the back of my leg, allowing me to get even closer, pressing every part of me into her.

I find a spot behind her neck that makes a soft sound vibrate from inside her throat. I send a row of kisses down the column of her neck before lifting my forehead to hers, wanting to gauge where she's at before we get too carried away. Her eyes flit up to meet mine, both of us out of breath.

She opens her mouth as if she's about to say something, and for a split second, I wonder and hope that maybe she might invite me in. But the slightest hesitation that she shows when she bites her lip instead of saying anything is all that I need to know. I smile and place a kiss right between her eyes before slowly disentangling myself from her.

"Goodnight, Tori," I say gruffly, stepping back, my body already protesting her absence.

"Goodnight, Connor." Rolling her lips, she attempts to hide a smile as she opens her door and gives me one last glance before closing it.

Without Tori to focus on, exhaustion becomes overwhelming, so I blow out a deep sigh, willing myself to stay awake while I walk back to the elevators to make my way home.

27

TORI

"Are you gonna eat all that?" I ask Connor, pointing to the barely touched tray of shrimp tacos and mango salsa that I had delivered to the office that are still sitting next to his keyboard. Typing away furiously, his eyes still locked on his laptop, it takes him a minute to register that I asked him a question.

"Huh? Oh, no, go ahead," he offers absentmindedly without so much as a glance my way.

I happily take one of his tacos, leaving two for him, and I bring it to my desk, taking a bite over my empty tray. My eyelids involuntarily drift shut in a moment of hunger and pure fatigue. I'm running on fumes at this point. We've both spent the day glued to our chairs, following up with gala guests, fielding calls from agents, and answering a million questions. This is the first time all day that I've stopped to even consider eating anything.

"Connor, you need to eat," I mumble between bites, knowing for a fact that he also hasn't eaten much either.

"Hm?" he distractingly asks.

"It's almost ten-thirty at night. Have you eaten anything more than a piece of gum all day?"

"You sound like my grandma," he says, still typing away.

"Thank you. I love your grandma," I say simply.

When he doesn't come back with a witty retort, I wipe my fingers and discard my napkin into the tray before pushing out of my chair. It's only when I very carefully move a stack of papers to the side and hoist myself to sit on his desk that he briefly flicks his eyes in my direction.

"Hey." I touch my fingertips to his forearm gently when he focuses back on his computer. "Do you want to take a little break?"

"I just need to email this recent inspection report…give me just one…minute." He taps the final key with purpose before sighing and leaning back in his chair. He brings his arms up to clasp his hands at the back of his neck. His face softens, and I can visibly see his tense features start to relax, starting with the disappearing creases around his eyes all the way down to the stretching of his legs.

"Hi," he says softly, piercing me with an intent look, the corner of his mouth starting to lift up. One thing that I'm discovering about Connor is that, while he gravitates toward focusing on work, he's able to shift his focus when he wants to and become completely in the moment with whatever it is that he's doing. He's looking at me with the same determination as he did at his laptop moments before, now fully present and open toward me.

"Hi," I say in return, a small smile forming of my own. Even though we've been two feet away from each other all day, I feel like this is the first time we're really seeing each other. The first time we're connecting. I grab the tray of tacos and hand it to him, a silent reminder to eat.

"These are really good," I tell him. He grabs the tray, taking a large bite, and I can tell by the look on his face that he agrees. I watch as he practically inhales the rest of the taco.

"So, any luck today?" he asks me between bites, keeping his eyes on me.

"I made a little headway for sure. One agent wants to bring his clients back through tomorrow to see it again, so I'll meet them around two, and then I think another agent might want to come the next day."

"Any word from Sarah and Micah?" he asks, setting the now empty tray on his desk.

"No, which is weird. I sent her a text right away this morning, and she never answered me. She usually responds right away, so this is odd."

"Really odd," he agrees.

"How about you?" I ask, placing the toe of my strappy sandal against the outside of his chair, letting it move back and forth as he slowly swivels.

"Roger definitely seemed interested. That's who I was sending the inspection report to. His clients are from New York. They plan on retiring within the next year and are looking to get out of the city. They want to get the most out of retirement that they possibly can."

"What a place to retire," I muse. "Makana would be perfect. Is it just the two of them?"

"Yeah, but apparently, they have a large extended family that they say will be visiting often."

"Awesome. Hopefully, they'll want to fly out to see it in person soon." Although, there are only two weeks left until the end of the year, so I know that it might be a long shot for that to happen before January.

"Oh, and I spoke with Tina, the videographer," I add. "She said she got plenty of good drone footage from the gala, and she should be able to make a video compilation within the next few days."

"Sweet. That'll be awesome to blast on social media. I hope she captured my good side in the video." He runs his hand down the left side of his face.

"You have a good side?" I tease, channeling some of his sarcasm.

"My mom tells me I do," he retorts with a shrug. When he smirks at me in a smug way, I push my lips together to hide my growing smile, suddenly unable to forget the way he looked yesterday in his tux. The memory of us slow dancing before the gala fills my mind, and I feel a shiver spread down my arms at how intimate the moment was. I felt a closeness with him in that moment that still takes my breath away when I think about it.

The sound of heels tapping on the floor shifts my attention up to see Beth walking down the aisle, a pile of manila folders in hand.

"Hey, Beth," I say with a surprised wave. "I didn't think anyone else was still here."

"Hey, guys." She slows when she reaches the wall of Connor's cubicle. "Late night, huh? I hear your gala went well last night."

"Yeah, it was great. You missed out," Connor replies with a kind smile.

"Sorry, I couldn't make it. I'm trying to wrap up this property near Haleiwa, and we had a planning meeting over there yesterday. I would have loved to come, though."

"No problem," I say as she shifts the folders in her arm.

"Oh, also, a little heads up. I have another client showing tomorrow evening at Makana Manor. A second showing. My clients from today want to see it again. I just updated the calendar," she says warmly before starting to walk away.

"Sounds good," I say, silently hoping that we make some progress with one of our potential buyers before her client would even have a chance to make an offer.

"Have a good night!" she calls before disappearing down the

aisle toward the exit. With a renewed surge of energy, I hop down and slide back into my chair, waking up my laptop with a swipe of my finger on the mouse pad. Connor walks to the break room that's just across the hallway. I find my gala paperwork to cross-reference the guests that I've already touched base with today. I'm just crossing a name off my list when he comes back to his desk.

"I took a peek at the calendar. It looks like Beth has her showing tomorrow evening, and then there's nothing on the calendar for the following two days. Rich has an open house planned for this Thursday."

"Well, let's keep working away, then," I say, getting back to my list. We work for another half hour, with the tapping of our keyboards the only sound that fills the office. Eventually, Connor shuts his computer with a yawn.

"Alright, I'm going to call it a night," he says.

"That's probably a good idea. I still only made a small dent in my follow-up list, though. I plan to come back early in the morning."

"I'll bring donuts and coffee," he says, holding out his hand to help me out of my chair. We tidy up our spaces a little bit and then walk out the front doors, exhausted but still fueled by plenty of adrenaline and anticipation of everything else that's left to do.

28

TORI

From: Brad@covestocondosrealty.com
To: You, and 45 others

Greetings everyone,

I have an update on the Makana Manor listing. If anyone is in the office this morning and is interested in hearing the update, I'll be in conference room two at eight-thirty. Again, this is not mandatory, I just wanted to offer an opportunity to bring everyone up to speed.

Have a great day!
Brad

My stomach instantly feels like a bowling ball just landed on it, and I sit up in my bed abruptly, a wave of messy hair falling over my eyes. Blowing it out of the way with an upward puff of air, I stare at my phone in shock. Does this mean someone brought an offer already? After all that work we put into the gala? I haven't even followed up with half of my guests yet, and I'm supposed to have a showing this afternoon. Is the owner taking it off the market? Ugh, it's eight o'clock now. Can I get to the office in time?

The flash of an incoming call interrupts my phone screen and my spiraling thoughts. Connor's name flashes on the screen, and a small rush of relief jolts through me just from seeing his name. I swipe to answer and hit the speaker option as I simultaneously jump out of my bed.

"Did you see the email?" Connor asks, his voice slightly muffled and distracted as if he's rummaging around like I am right now too.

"What do you think it means? An offer already? Who could have brought one to the table?" I set the phone on top of my bathroom countertop and quickly pull my hair back into a bun. I squeeze some toothpaste on my toothbrush and screw the cap back on.

"Do you think it was Beth? I know she had interested clients. She had that showing last week, too," I say, shoving the toothbrush in my mouth, not bothering to wait until after the conversation to brush my teeth. "But she didn't mention it last night."

"Who knows? I guess we'll find out at the meeting. I'll meet you at the office?"

"Save me a seat, please," I say in a rush, hanging up and shedding my clothes to jump in the shower. After the fastest shower of my life, I slip into a black pencil skirt and a sleeveless purple blouse before running a quick brush through my hair. I debate the necessity of makeup but end up throwing on a coat of mascara and blush to look at least a little bit polished. I never know what the span of a day will bring, so it's best to be prepared. I don't even bother to give myself one last glance before scurrying to the kitchen.

I make a super quick latte, then set my travel coffee mug on the counter next to the growing pile of Christmas cards that no longer fit on my display wall, but I can't quite bring myself to throw away. Once my heels are strapped on, I grab everything I need and head out the door in a rush.

At the office, I pass straight by my cubicle altogether and immediately make a beeline down the hallway to conference room two, where Brad's just about to shut the door.

"I'm here, I'm here," I say, squeezing past. I do a quick scan and find Connor waving near the front row of chairs, so I head in his direction and slide into the empty chair next to him.

"Saving that sock for later?" he asks, pointing to my skirt, where a white ankle sock is pressed firmly to the side of it.

"Oh my gosh." I snatch it off and shove it in my purse, ignoring his low chuckle. "It's been a morning, okay?"

"Alright," Brad starts, making his way to the front of the room. "I want to start by saying thank you to everyone who's been working on this listing to help me out. I know that many of you have gone to great lengths to find a buyer. Your hard work has not gone unnoticed, and I appreciate every one of you and your efforts."

"Here it comes," Connor whispers.

"Now for the update. We officially have an offer that was presented late last night on Makana Manor, and my client has since accepted."

My heart drops for the second time this morning as my suspicions are officially confirmed.

"I want to say a quick congratulations to Rich for being the agent to bring me the offer."

A few pathetic claps are heard around the room as disgust swirls in my gut. Rich comes to stand next to Brad, and the smug look on his face only further induces nausea. He's more irritating to me at this moment than he ever has been before.

"Ugh," I say quietly to Connor, disappointment weighing heavy on my chest that matches the look on his face. "This sucks."

"I know." He gives my leg a gentle nudge with his knee. "Majorly."

"I won't keep you much longer," Brad says. "I just wanted to keep you all informed so you know the status of the listing. There will be no further open houses or advertising necessary as Makana Manor is officially in escrow. Please cancel any upcoming showings you may have on the calendar. Have a great day, everyone."

Chairs are pushed back, and people start chatting as they make their way out of the room. With a heavy sigh, I reluctantly stand. As I follow Connor through the rows of chairs, I can't help but overhear Brad as he hands a piece of paper to Rich.

"I just have one more thing for you to have Sarah and Micah sign. Have them fax it back to me by this afternoon."

A slow, ominous shiver runs across the top of my skin, and I feel like I just ran into a wall. For the first time in my life, I seriously wonder if there's actual steam coming out of my ears. Anger and disbelief consume me, so much so that there's a slight ringing in my ears, and I get tunnel vision as I rush past Connor and down the hall to my cubicle. Could it be? There's no way, right? There's no way he's talking about MY Sarah and Micah, right?

I slam down into my chair and power up my computer, desperate for any sort of answer that I can find. I don't have any missed phone calls on my phone, but when I sign into my work email, I see it. An email from Sarah, sent an hour ago with the heading of *I'm so sorry*.

From: SarahG@gmail.com

To: You

Tori, I don't really know how else to say this, so I'll just come right out and say it. We have decided to move forward with another agent on the Makana Manor property. It's absolutely nothing personal. I so appreciate your help and the time you put into helping us with our property search. Truly, it means the world to me. I'm so sorry it came down to this, but I do wish you nothing but the best in the future.

Regards,
Sarah

"What in the…" I don't realize that I've said the words out loud until Connor's chair bumps mine as he shifts in his seat. I blink away my fog and find him next to me, staring expectantly.

"What?" he asks in a way that has me sure it isn't the first time he's asked.

"He stole them," is all I can push out through the stream of angry words and accusations that are filling my mind.

"Who stole who?" A crease deepens between his eyes in confusion.

"Rich. He stole Sarah and Micah."

"What? How is that possible?"

"I don't know, but he did. Sarah just sent me an apology email."

"Wow," he says, running his hand over his jaw in anger before lightly grabbing the back of my elbow. "Are you okay?"

I will the tears to not come as I nod. I'm used to rejection and deals falling through in our line of work—that's just part of the business. But this feels different. This whole thing felt like way more than just a sale or a silly competition to me. It was more like a status-cementing deal within the company, which I didn't realize I had needed so badly until now. It was confirmation.

Security. Direction for the future, maybe. All of it is gone now, along with the listing.

"Yeah, I'm okay. It just stings," I say quietly.

"I know," he says, blowing out a rough sigh before standing up. "Let's go get ice cream."

"What?" I say with a weak laugh. "It's eight-forty-five in the morning. And you brought donuts."

"It is. And I did. But if there was ever a better time for a macadamia caramel cone, then I don't know when that would be."

With a half-hearted smile and another sigh, I push myself out of my chair, more than ready to get some fresh air.

"Okay," I agree, walking in front of him. "But you're buying.

29

CONNOR

"One dairy-free chocolate-chip scoop for the pretty lady," I say, holding the Styrofoam cup out to Tori. "Although, you can't possibly tell me cashew milk ice cream actually tastes good."

I lower myself onto the picnic table next to Tori on the seat closest to the street, placing a leg on either side of the bench and angling myself toward her. The ice cream stand we walked to sits along the side of the road just down the street from our office building, which I can see from here. A large crowd is already gathering around the stand, regardless of the early hour. The sun is already hot, not a cloud in the sky, and a steady stream of cars rush past us in the direction of the beach.

"It tastes very good, actually. You want a bite?" She thrusts a spoonful to my lips before she's even taken a bite of it herself. Sliding it off the spoon with my mouth, I take the bite and nod my head slowly.

"Not terrible," I admit with a shrug. "Not great, but not terrible."

She smiles, and my chest warms, knowing I made her even just a tiny bit happy, especially when I know how much disappointment is hiding under the surface. Losing the competition was a huge blow for both of us. It's devastating to lose it all in the blink of an eye. So much of my focus has been on that listing for the last several weeks, and it's jarring to have it all taken away in a split second. But even so, what I'm most aware of right now is that I'm experiencing more than just disappointment. I'm also feeling helpless and protective in wanting to make sure that Tori is okay.

I have a strong urge to make her smile and do anything I can to cheer her up. The recognition of that makes me feel a little uneasy, as it just proves how hard I really am falling for her, but I push those thoughts to the side, not wanting to give them any more attention and unnecessarily freak myself out.

"Why would they do that? Submit an offer with Rich? It doesn't make any sense," she says as I take a bite of my own ice cream.

"I have no idea, but I wouldn't put it past Rich to use some sneaky tactics to secure a deal."

"Ugh." She pouts, sticking her lower lip out.

"'Ugh,' is right." I run my hand along her spine through her blouse, then gently squeeze at her shoulder. "For what it's worth, I'm glad we ended up teaming up on this. I'm proud of what we accomplished in such a short amount of time, even if there's nothing to show for it now."

She gives me a half-smile. "I'm proud of us too."

We spend a few quiet minutes drowning our sorrows in ice cream before she turns to me. "Anyway, do you have anything else going on the rest of the day? I know we were planning on another busy day with follow-ups at the office," she says, bringing the spoon to her mouth.

"I actually have a last-minute listing appointment in about a half hour. They called on my way into the office." I check my watch. "I should probably get going soon, actually. How about you?"

"Nothing too crazy. I guess my day has been cleared now. I have a closing scheduled for tomorrow, so I do need to get a few last-minute things done for that. Otherwise, I'll probably just spend the day at my desk. I suppose I should let the other interested agents know that Makana is officially in escrow."

"Yeah, that's on my list too." I scrape the last bite of my melted ice cream out of the cup. "Do you want me to walk you back to the office?"

"No. You go ahead," she says.

"Are you sure?"

"I can handle the short walk. I survived just fine on my own before—this started, you know." She waves her hand between us before smiling.

"If you insist," I say, matching her smile. "I'll call you after my appointment?"

When she nods her head, I lift up but hover halfway to plant a kiss on the side of her head, half of my lips on her hair and the other half on her skin. With a final squeeze of her arm, I throw our garbage in the trash and head off toward my car after a final wave.

The entire ride there, my thoughts are consumed with the amount of time and money that we've essentially wasted the last few weeks. Although losing listings to other agents is absolutely commonplace in our industry, it's never easy to have one slip through your hands so suddenly—especially one with such a high reward and benefits. A part of me feels a little lost now that I no longer have the listing to strive for.

When I pull into my potential client's two-story home in the middle of Honolulu, I clear my thoughts and pull myself together. Walking up the stone walkway, I scan the white and wood exterior of the home. I step onto the small front porch area and knock on the door.

"Connor, nice to meet you," an older gentleman says, opening the front door wide.

"Pat, my pleasure." I shake his hand. "You have a beautiful home."

"Thank you, come on in." I follow him inside, stopping in the entryway as he shuts the front door behind me.

"So you're thinking of listing, huh? Are you planning on moving somewhere else?" I ask.

"I am interested in listing," he confirms. "My wife passed away six months ago, and it's just me now. I can't keep up with the maintenance of it, and I certainly don't need all the room."

"I'm sorry for your loss," I say sympathetically.

"Thank you. So I'm looking to downsize. Long story short, I'd love to wait until after Christmas to officially list, but I wanted to get your thoughts and opinions on price and all that."

"I can do that. I'd love for you to show me around."

"You got it."

I follow him all the way inside, where he takes me on a tour around the twenty-six-hundred-square-foot home with plenty of recently updated renovations and decent quality appliances. I walk through the kitchen and take mental notes on the space as I scan the room.

It's a nice house—easily a one-point-four-million-dollar listing, but it doesn't quite hold the same appeal as it would have a month ago for me. It's almost like I need that big listing or something huge to aspire toward. Otherwise, it almost feels like something is missing. I tap my hand on the kitchen island and force myself to refocus.

"Looks great. I love the layout of this main area. Open floor plans are a huge selling point for buyers. Show me upstairs?" I ask.

He leads me upstairs, where the primary bedroom is located,

plus three other smaller bedrooms and a shared bathroom. Outside one of the bedroom windows, I get a glimpse of the spacious backyard.

"I think a family with children is going to be the buyer for your house. This place is excellent for kids."

"Once upon a time, it was full of my own kids," he says, nostalgia heavy in his voice. "Time to pass it on to some new ones."

"We'll find the perfect buyer," I promise. "So, how soon after the holidays are you wanting to put it on the market?"

"Pretty soon after, if you've got room in your schedule," he says. "I'm moving into an apartment on the other side of town the week after Christmas, so it would be empty at that point."

"Great. We can figure out details later, such as staging costs and a solid plan, but this is a good start. Let me run some comps in the neighborhood, and I'll get in touch this afternoon so we can talk price. How does that sound?"

"Sounds like a plan," he says. I follow him down the stairs, and even though I'm ready to get back to the office and let this listing as well as my other active ones take my mind off of Makana, there's still a lingering disappointment and emptiness that stays with me as I head back outside. Unfortunately for me, it also lasts the entire rest of the day.

30

TORI

"That was so much fun," I tell Connor, looping my arm with his as we walk out of the Hawaii Theatre's main doors and onto the streets of downtown Honolulu that are filling with a swarm of other people that are trickling out of the theater.

"You want my honest thoughts?" he asks, giving me a side-eye.

"Of course," I reply chipperly.

"You are the only person in this entire world that I would sit in a crowded theater for and watch a grown man sing for two hours."

I laugh, feeling honored and amused at the same time. "This was your idea, you know," I point out.

Truth be told, I was excited when Connor asked me on another date and said that he got tickets for the Christmas-themed performance. Watching local performers sing traditional Hawaiian songs was just what I needed to get my mind out of the slump that I've been in ever since Rich stole our buyers two days ago. Although the initial sting has worn off slightly, a cloud of despondency has been lingering over me ever since.

"I don't think it was one of my better ideas. I can think of about a million other semi-productive things that we should have done." He cringes with a laugh. "But I'm glad you enjoyed it."

"I did." I squeeze his arm tighter and take in the colorful lights that are strung throughout the trees, illuminating and lining the streets with lights, the picturesque scene getting me even more in the holiday spirit.

"I can't believe Christmas is next week," I say a little breathily.

"This last month has flown, hasn't it?"

"It really has," I agree. "How are you feeling about work?"

He shrugs, bringing my arms with him as he lifts his shoulders. "Alright...not great. Honestly, I'm feeling a little bit lost."

"Are you?" I swing my head up to look at him, surprised that he didn't give me a generic, basic answer.

"I mean, it's not like I'm not busy enough. Business and workload have never been an issue. But ever since losing Makana, it's like there's something missing. I was really thriving when I was working toward the prestige of selling that estate, you know? I wanted that title. And not for vanity reasons, just simply to advance a little bit. Move forward. I didn't realize it until now, but I think I'm feeling a little bit stuck professionally."

"Really? I never would have guessed that's how you've been feeling. Why didn't you say something?"

"It's not a big deal." He shrugs once again.

"It is, though, if that's how you feel."

"Yeah. I don't know. I'll keep thinking about it." He brushes me off. "Sorry for the purge. I had a lot of time to think during the concert."

Spotting his car close by, I slide in front of him when we

reach it before he has a chance to open my door for me. With a sly smile, I pull him in for a hug and wrap my arms around his waist before looking up at him.

"I like when you purge your thoughts. I like knowing what's going on up there. And thank you for tonight," I say softly, unable to look away from his eyes, which crinkle together when he smiles back at me.

"You're very welcome," he says, clasping his hands around my lower back. Once again, I find comfort in the way I feel when I'm in his arms. Safe. Seen. Adored.

It's now very obvious to me how attached I've become to him. How I gravitate to being with him as much as possible and how much I miss him when we're apart. Those realizations stay at the forefront of my thoughts when I look up at him.

"Do you want to come back to my place? For a nightcap?" I ask and then watch the slow progression of his smile.

"I'd love to," he says a mere second before pressing his lips to mine. He gives me a chaste, respectful peck before pulling away, leaving me craving more. He gives me a knowing smirk as if he can read my mind, while he reaches around me and opens the car door, then gently shuts it behind me once I'm in.

Back at my condo, Connor insists on sending me straight out to the balcony while he gets us two glasses of wine from my kitchen. Not one to argue, I pull the blanket out of the basket on my way out and nestle it over me, settling into one of my chairs with my legs bent and off to my side.

"Ma'am," he says, holding the wine glass out for me. I don't think I do a good job of hiding my immediate repulsion at his words.

"Yeah, that sounded wrong the second it came out," he says, to which I chuckle. "My lady? Is that better?"

"Tori is fine," I insist with an eye roll.

He sets his wine glass and his phone next to mine on the small table between the chairs, then settles onto the empty chair.

I can't help but keep my gaze on him instead of the view down below, and I watch as he folds his arms across his chest when a slightly cool breeze of ocean air sweeps through.

"Are you cold?" I ask.

"Nah, I'm good," he says, but his biceps flinch as he squeezes his arms a little bit tighter.

Not pleased with that answer, I curl the blanket around me and shuffle over to where he's sitting, and gesture for him to separate his legs. I have a seat between them and then lean back so the back of my head is on his chest, just under his chin, and I lay the blanket over both of us.

"Better?" I ask.

"Besides your boney elbows, yes," he teases while wrapping his strong arms around me.

I shake my head in amusement, wondering how we've come to this comfortable place in such a short amount of time. Just over a month ago, Connor was just my work friend and cubicle-mate. My confidant and go-to person when it came to discussing anything work-related. And now I'm realizing that he's somehow quickly becoming my go-to person in all aspects of my life.

His phone buzzes on the table next to us, and he doesn't move a muscle to answer it.

"So, how do you think we've been handling this whole dating situation?" I ask quietly when the buzzing stops, genuinely curious to hear how he's feeling about us. "And balancing work life? Do you think we're doing okay?"

I can feel his chest rise and fall as he takes a deep breath. I half expect a sarcastic response, but instead, I get one with nothing but sincerity.

"I think we're doing great." His voice comes out husky and laced with emotion. It's distinct enough that I sit up and twist around to face him.

"Yeah?" I pry for more. He meets my gaze, wrapping his fingers gently around my wrist that's perched on top of the chair.

"Yeah." With a nod, he tugs gently on my arm to pull me closer. I shift, and soon we're completely rearranged so that I'm straddling him on the chair with my hands loose on top of his shoulders and my thighs pressed firmly against his. My feet are behind me, my toes tucked under his legs.

"You're not sick of me yet?" I ask quietly, starkly aware of the buzzing energy that's quickly ramping up between us. He reaches an arm up to tuck some hair behind my ear. I watch him as his gaze follows the movement of his hand, outlining my face.

"Surprisingly, no," he says gruffly, pushing his lips together in a contemplative half-smile. He flicks his eyes back to mine, piercing with intensity.

"In fact, I want more." He swallows and rolls his lips before pulling me in closer until I'm hovering above his face. "I need more. I'm all in, Tori—if you'll have me, that is."

I hover where I am for a few seconds, taking in the weight of his words and this consuming energy. Then I answer by leaning forward and pressing my lips to his. Bringing my hands to his jawline, I cup his face and slide my fingers into his hair.

"I'm all in, too," I murmur against his mouth between kisses, and he grips my hip with one hand and places the other at my rib cage. He pushes himself forward to sit up until we're vertical, upright, and pressed together, showing each other the intensity of our feelings without using words.

When I'm with him in this way, there's absolutely no sign of timid, nervous Connor. No insecurities or hesitation at all in his movements. Confidence and steady control is all that oozes from him, and I get high off of it.

He pulls away and moves his mouth to the spot right below my ear that sends a tingle all the way down my spine. That's when his phone buzzes on the table again.

"Do you need to get that?" I whisper, letting my head fall to the side.

"No," he says against my neck before pulling back to look me in the eyes. It dawns on me that, even though he was just saying earlier that he needed more from work, he still chooses to set it aside for me.

A silent understanding passes between us, and when I give him a slight nod, he slides both of his arms under my butt and hoists us up. I wrap my ankles around each other behind Connor's waist and kiss him again as he carries us back inside toward my room, leaving his phone buzzing on the table.

31

———————

CONNOR

I fumble through Tori's cupboards in search of her coffee mugs. The edge of the counter feels cool against my shirtless torso when I find them and reach for two mugs. I get everything prepped, and while I wait for the coffee to brew, I tuck my hands into yesterday's shorts pockets, my mind drifting to last night and how incredible it was. The date. The balcony. The connection. All of it was so incredibly amazing.

I still can't believe where we're at with each other and how it's been a mostly comfortable transition into a romantic relationship between us, which is completely baffling to me. If someone would have told me, even a few months ago, that I would be in a committed relationship by Christmas, I wouldn't have believed it. Not with my dating track record and uncanny ability to make even the slightest romantic situations awkward. I wouldn't have believed it for a second.

My eye catches on the large pile of Christmas cards on the

counter. The one on the top says *Happy Holidays from The Parkers*, with a picture of a family posing, the view of the Golden Gate Bridge in the background. I smile, thinking of how sweet Elliot was to sign her up for this. I'm glad he was looking out for her. But if I have anything to say about it, her family won't have to worry about her being lonely anymore.

I fill the two mugs with coffee just as Tori comes shuffling down the hallway, wearing black biker shorts and an oversized teal sweatshirt. Her thick hair is unkempt and disheveled, and I bite back a laugh at how adorable she looks.

"Morning," she says groggily, rubbing her eye with her sweatshirt sleeve.

"Morning, sunshine." I pass a mug to her, which she graciously takes, and then I follow her outside to the balcony.

"Sleep okay?" she asks, dropping into a chair. I sit in the opposite chair and take a sip of my coffee, taking in the view in the daylight. The sun is sitting just above the palm trees, a faint line of dark orange and cherry red extending out before disappearing into a bright-blue sky. A sunrise aerobics class is taking place down at the pool, and faint Christmas music can be heard coming from a speaker on the pool deck. The air somehow feels cool and humid at the same time, waiting for the sun to finish rising and take the chill away completely.

"Other than your snoring keeping me up, it was great," I can't resist teasing.

"I. Do. Not. Snore," she protests, looking offended.

"I'm pretty sure you were unconscious, so you wouldn't know."

Tori's phone buzzes with a notification, and when she rolls her eyes at my comment and pulls it out, I go with the moment and grab mine out of my pocket too.

We spend a few minutes answering emails in a comfortable quiet, getting a head start on the never-ending tasks, despite the fact that it's the weekend. I text Pat, the homeowner from the listing appointment the other day, and give him a checklist of things I recommend he do to get his house showing ready before we put it on the market.

"What are your plans for the day?" Tori asks, eventually setting her phone down on the table.

"I just have a builders meeting later this afternoon. Nothing too crazy. You?"

"I actually don't have any client meetings set up for today. I think things are going to start slowing down for a little bit here. The few days before Christmas tend to be on the slower side for me while people settle in to enjoy the holidays with their families."

I nod in agreement before she continues on.

"But it is Sunday, and my family always meets for lunch at my parents' house, so I'll go to that today." She smiles and curls her sweatshirt over her fingers, readjusting the mug in her hand.

"Do you mind if I come with you?" I spit out, acting on the sudden unrelenting urge to spend as much time together as we can.

"You want to willingly spend time with my loud and nosy family?" Her brows lift in disbelief, but I don't miss the way her eyes light up.

"I like your family," I chuckle. "And I like you even more."

She brings her coffee mug to her face, attempting to hide her blush and smile behind it before shrugging. "It's your choice. I'd love to bring you if you think you can handle the constant questions and tiresome commentary."

I return a shrug of my own. "I handle you just fine."

She leans over and slaps me on the shoulder for that one, causing a slapping sound to ring out over my laugh.

"Sorry, it was too easy," I apologize. She sets her mug down and comes over to me, leaning down to give me a kiss.

"I'll get you back for that one, but I need to shower," she

says, walking to the balcony door before giving me a backward glance.

"You coming?"

"Something's different," Grace says with a skeptical look, waving her hand between Tori and me. We've been at Tori's parents' house for all of six minutes, and I feel a little bit like we're the subject of a firing squad. Having met everyone at the parade, I feel mostly comfortable around her family, but there's a tiny sense of uneasiness as I know how unpredictable and unrelenting her sisters can be. It wouldn't surprise me if they could somehow sense that Tori and I slept together last night.

"I can't put my finger on it, but there's definitely something different. Did you cut your hair?" Grace asks Tori.

"Nope," she replies simply, moving past the wall of sisters into the kitchen, seemingly unaffected.

"Is this romper new?" Emily asks, waving her hand over Tori's outfit.

"Nope. Do you want something to drink, Connor?" Tori asks, turning back to me.

"Of course he does," Matt answers for me, pulling a beer from the fridge and holding it out in my direction.

"Thanks." I graciously accept it, coming to stand next to Tori, who's leaning against the kitchen island.

"Did Matt tell you guys why we were late coming over here today?" Paige asks, thankfully changing the subject.

"No, why?" Ava asks, settling back around the island.

"He planned the cutest Christmas-themed family date for all four of us this morning," she gushes. "We woke up super early and went all over the island."

"Fun! What did you do?" Emily asks.

"We toured the Christmas sand sculptures at the Sheraton,

then took photos with Santa, and got some last-minute gifts at the International Market Place. Then we rounded out the eventful morning with ice skating at the convention center. It was cute. He even made a little laminated checklist for Elliot."

"Aw, Matt," Grace gushes, "you're still so good at planning that kind of stuff."

"He is. We trained you well, didn't we?" Emily pats the top of his head.

"What am I, a dog?" Matt asks, completely unaffected by their teasing.

"No, but you are a cute little specimen of a man that we spent years molding and shaping," Grace teases.

I watch in amusement as Matt stands up, pushing his stool back in.

"Please don't use the words cute and little in a sentence to describe me. It's highly inaccurate." He opens the sliding deck door behind him. "Come on, Connor. It's less annoying out here."

Tori gives me a 'save yourself' nod, so I happily follow him out the door and onto the deck, where Elliot is drawing at the table under an umbrella with Tori's mom.

"Connor, it's so nice to see you again. Have a seat," she says with a welcoming smile. "Elliot was just teaching me how to draw a 3D dragon."

"Atta boy. That's a life skill right there," Matt says. I take the chair next to him, scooting my chair in between him and Elliot.

"Hi, Connor," Elliot says, briefly looking up from his sketch pad.

"Hey, Elliot. I like that dragon." I point to his drawing. "Are you excited for Christmas?"

He nods his head vigorously. "Yes! It's my very favorite holiday."

"What's on your Christmas list?" I ask, taking a sip of my beer.

"A puppy," Elliot and Matt answer at the same time.

"Oh, that's a big one," I say with a laugh.

"It's really the only thing I want," Elliot says as Tori's mom stands up.

"Well, you've definitely been on the nice list, sweetie, so fingers crossed," she says, ruffling Elliot's hair. "Excuse me, gentlemen, I'm going to go get started on the food."

I give her a polite nod as she walks behind me back into the house, and I take a sip of my beer. Out of the corner of my eye, I can see Matt giving me a once-over, from top to bottom, pausing a little too long on my face.

"So, Connor," he starts, and I brace myself for what he's about to say. "What are your intentions with my sister?"

I clear my throat, growing uncomfortable under his stare, which has no trace of the friendliness that it just had a moment earlier.

"Listen, I really like your sister—" I start, fidgeting with my hands.

"Oh, for Pete's sake," Tori interrupts as she walks outside. "Really, Matt?"

"Hey, I'm just doing my job as your brother," he responds with a shrug, eyes still locked on me.

"Well, stop, please." Tori grabs the chair across from me.

"I seem to remember all of you meddling in my dating life too. It's what we do. We look out for each other."

"It's not necessary this time," she says to him, shooting me a soft smile, which I return, holding her gaze. A sense of calm begins to overshadow the twinge of discomfort of the conversation at hand. Matt looks back and forth between us before leaning back in his chair, seemingly satisfied.

"If you say so. Just don't let me have to give you the rest of the spiel, okay?"

"You have nothing to worry about, man. I promise." I give him a sincere nod.

"Then we're good," he replies before focusing back on Elliot. "Hey, Elliot, what was your favorite part of our family date this morning?"

"Ice skating," he replies, still happily sketching away. "It reminded me of Minnesota."

We spend the next half hour chatting with Elliot about all things dragons, puppies, and his favorite snow activities before heading inside for lunch. All the while, I let my guard all the way down and acknowledge the lingering sense of peace that I feel around Tori's family and the small voice in the back of my head telling me that I fit in here.

32

TORI

"Okay, just one last thing," I say as I send over a purchase agreement via email to the local title company. I'm hunched forward over my laptop that's positioned on top of the brand-new coffee table in Connor's living room. The coffee table that he bought this afternoon, and still has the tag on.

"Take your time," he says from beside me, his fingers working away on his own phone.

"I'm done." I close my laptop with a sigh, leaning back, my arm pressing against his. He follows a second behind me and lays his phone on the table. My gaze drifts to the small additions that Connor has made to his place, namely the cozy rug that was on display with the coffee table at the store and the floor lamp in the corner opposite his Christmas tree. However, even with the additions, his tree still looks ridiculously bare without a single ornament on it, which somehow still seems fitting and makes me smile.

"Ready to go?" He squeezes my knee, shifting to stand before offering me a hand.

"Ready." I nod, rising and letting my hand linger against his for a moment before reaching for the beach bag that I brought with me when I left the office today. "I just need to change quickly."

"Don't forget your arm floaties. I make no promises on my paddle boarding abilities," Connor says as I pull my swimsuit out of my bag. Slapping him on the butt with my clothes as I pass, I change into my black two-piece swimsuit, then pull on a pair of ripped jean shorts. I slide my arms through a white button-down shirt, leaving it unbuttoned so it serves as a cover-up.

Back in the kitchen, I find Connor taking a few water bottles out of the fridge. He comes around the side of the island, and I throw the water bottles into my beach bag. He slides an arm between my open shirt and grips my bare side, gently squeezing while kissing my temple, lingering there.

"Mmm. Don't start something we can't finish," I tell him softly when he moves his hand around my back, finding a new resting place on the back of my hips.

"Who says we can't finish?" he mumbles into my hair.

"Me," I say, turning to wrap my arms around him. "You promised me a paddle board ride before sunset." I give him a quick kiss before twisting out of his embrace, pulling my beach bag onto my shoulder.

"Blah," he says, his eyes telling me that he would completely abandon that plan in a heartbeat.

"Come on, it'll be fun!" I grab his hand with a smile and lead him out into his garage, where the paddle-board that we borrowed from Matt and Paige is leaning against the wall. I grab the paddle while he grabs the board, positioning it under his arm before we start the walk down his street. I admire the quaint beach-y homes that line his neighborhood as we quickly come up to a path between two houses that leads to the next street over.

"What a sweet little neighborhood you live in," I say as we walk along the narrow dirt path that's peppered with bushes and greenery.

"Thank you," he says, his voice dripping in sarcasm. "That's exactly what I was going for when I bought my house. A sweet little neighborhood."

"Well, mission accomplished." We reach pavement and turn left down the street, heading in the direction of the sign sticking out of the dirt that reads *Beach Access.* We walk along while I admire the houses—one a salmon-pink color with white trim, and another light-blue one that has a tall staircase leading up to a wrap-around porch.

"I miss Makana," I say quietly, glancing at Connor.

"Yeah?" he asks, turning his head toward me.

"Yeah." I nod. "I got attached to that house. Not in a possessive way. I never saw it as mine, of course, but I knew every nook and cranny of that place. I was invested in it, you know?"

"I know," he agrees softly. "I was too."

"It just feels like there was no closure. I would have loved to see the process all the way through and finalize the sale of it," I say as we take the beach access trail, my feet sinking into sand. I slip off my flip-flops and slide them into my bag. "At the end of the day, I just hope Sarah and Micah will be happy there."

"I'm sure they will be." Connor wraps his free arm around my shoulder. We walk to an open section of the busy beach and set our stuff down in the sand. There are groups of people clustered everywhere, as we've had a surge of tourists come into town for the holidays.

"Do you want to go out right away or sit and enjoy the view for a little while?" Connor asks, taking the paddle from me and gently setting it across the board.

"I have a better idea," I say with a grin that I can hardly hold inside.

"Why does that make me nervous?" he asks cautiously.

I sift through my beach bag and pull out a baseball and two gloves, both of which I also borrowed from Matt.

"That was in your bag?" he asks, a slow smile spreading on his face.

"Yup." I hand him a glove. "I remember you saying you used to play baseball as a kid and that if you had more time out of work you would probably make more time for sports. Well, here we are. Go sports! I thought playing catch would be fun—although I can't promise anything when it comes to my throw."

He slides his sunglasses on top of his head, allowing me to watch his eyes roam from the ball to the gloves and finally up to me. He walks closer, placing his hand on my hip.

"You"—he plants a kiss against my lips—"are amazing."

"Go long," I reply as he jogs a little ways before turning around to face me. I toss my button-up shirt on the sand and then slide my hand into a glove that feels a little bit too big. I throw the ball to Connor, who catches it easily, although he does have to lunge for it. He throws it back, and the ball bounces off the tip of my glove, landing in the sand and rolling off to the side. I pick it up, throw it back to a smiling Connor, and soak in how happy he looks.

We play catch for several minutes, being careful not to throw close to other beach dwellers. I feel proud that the aim of my throws improves with each pass. Eventually, we come to meet in the middle, tossing the gloves and ball on the sand.

"Nice job." He holds his hand up for a high-five, which I happily return.

"Alright, what do you say we get out there before the sun goes down," he says, lifting his shirt off, revealing his chiseled abs and defined arm muscles. I twist my hair up into a topknot and shimmy out of my shorts. Then I grab the paddle while

Connor carries the board, and we make our way to the edge of the water.

My first step into the ocean is cool, a refreshing reprieve from the stickiness of the humid air. The water splashes against my shins while I lift my legs higher, fighting the force of the waves as we step farther in.

"Alright, hop on," Connor says, flattening the board along the top of the water. He holds it steady as I lift my leg onto the board, pushing myself on top. Trying to keep myself steady, I sit on the front half, my legs criss-crossed, holding the paddle across my lap.

"Okay, I'll try my best not to dunk us," Connor says.

"What?" I whip my head around as he uses his arms to hoist himself up.

"Kidding," he mutters nonchalantly, focused on climbing aboard. "Kind of."

I grip the sides of the board and squeal as it wobbles under his shifting weight.

"There we go." He comes to a stand behind me, and I twist slightly to hand him the paddle. He pushes the paddle into the water, and with a strong shove, we surge ahead, my stomach dipping as we crest over the top of a small wave. Each stroke gets more and more fluid and has more control, pushing us farther out.

I bend my legs with my feet flat on the board, putting my arms straight out behind me to hold me up while Connor stands behind me and paddles us forward. The water is as pristine as glass, the lowering sun reflecting off the top, making it glisten with an orange-ish hue.

We make it out a little ways, Connor somehow expertly guiding us through the deep water. Eventually, he stops to take a break from paddling, and I twist my top half, watching him as he wipes the sweat off his forehead with his forearm.

"You sure you haven't done this before?" I ask. "You're actually really good at this. Like, really, really good."

"I haven't, but I like this vote of confidence. What else you got?" He slowly lowers to set the paddle horizontally along the board and brings his hands to his hips.

"Let's see. You're unbelievably smart and funny. And you're sexy as heck in those swim trunks," I say cheekily.

"It's the blue, isn't it?" He points to his dark-blue swim trunks.

"Obviously," I laugh. Before he can add another comment, I feel a stray drop of rain hit the top of my cheek right under my eye.

"Oh no. I hope it won't rain," I say, scanning the rapidly darkening sky. A questionable-looking cloud seems to have appeared suddenly and unexpectedly, as it often does here in December.

"Uh-oh," Connor says just as another drop hits his arm. Then another one hits my shoulder. And another. All of a sudden, we're right in the middle of a spontaneous rain shower while balancing on a paddle-board in the middle of the ocean.

"Ahh!" I squeal, the rain splattering against my whole body and bouncing off the board. I try and shield my face at first, but eventually, I give in to it and hang my head back, holding my arms out to the side, letting the cold rain hit my face. I peel my eyes open to peek at Connor, where he's standing, unaffected, rain-water dripping off his face, staring at me with a fire burning behind his eyes.

"What?" I ask with a laugh that gets swallowed up by the sound of the rain. He doesn't answer, but his eyes soften, and the next thing I know, he leans forward and grips the side of my head, moving in closer so he hovers over me, bringing his mouth to mine, connecting our lips upside down.

He kisses me, and I can feel the rain sliding down his face and melding with mine, unsure of where the raindrops first begin and where they end. The board starts wobbling, and he reluctantly breaks away to re-stabilize us.

I bring my head and angle it all the way down, shaking my hair back and forth. And then, just as suddenly as the rainstorm came, it passes just as quickly, and we're left with a darkening sky, completely soaked to the bone. Adrenaline still surges through me, and I take a few deep breaths to calm my heart rate, completely unsure if I'm so affected by the rainstorm or from the thrill of the kiss.

"Let me get you back in," Connor says finally, using the paddle to turn us around and expertly lead us back to shore.

33

CONNOR

"I'm going to fill up my coffee mug," I tell Tori as I lift out of my desk chair.

"Oh, if you bring me back one of those mini muffins that Cheryl brought in today, I wouldn't hate that," she replies with a smile, eyes still glued to her laptop.

"You got it." I walk the few steps it takes to reach the break room and head directly toward the coffee corner. After filling my mug with the carafe, I open the fridge in search of my favorite coffee creamer that I brought in on Monday.

"Brooks," Rich's voice booms from behind me as he strides into the room. Tension grips me as I slowly shut the fridge, trying to simmer the anger that just consumed me at his mere presence. I've been successfully avoiding him ever since the announcement about Makana, leaving me to brew over what happened. I've envisioned what I would say to him when I finally saw him in person, but none of that comes to mind now that we're here.

"Rich," I reply, not bothering to hide the disgust in my voice.

"Beautiful day, isn't it?"

I don't humor him with a response as he saunters over to the counter where half-empty packages of donuts and muffins are stacked on top of each other, next to foil-covered plates of homemade Christmas cookies and other goodies we get sent this time of year. He pulls out a sugar cookie and takes a bite before turning to me.

"Hey, no hard feelings about the listing, right?" His arrogance is palpable and sends a wave of nausea rolling through me.

"I don't have anything to say about Makana, Rich," I say dryly. I debate grilling him for information and giving him a piece of my mind, but at the end of the day, I decide there's no point in arguing over it. I'm mature enough to be professional about this, and I'm not one to hold a grudge—but it will definitely take some time before the sting of this betrayal completely fades.

"Suit yourself," he says, making his way out the door. "Wasn't personal."

"I couldn't wait," Tori says, coming into the break room before pausing briefly at the sight of Rich. My eyes flick to hers, searching for any sign of discomfort. To my amusement, she continues past him, not even slightly acknowledging him as he walks out of the room. When Rich is officially gone, she turns her nose up in disgust.

"Ugh," is all she has to say as she heads straight for the mini muffins.

"I was going to bring you a blueberry one," I tell her, leaning a hip against the counter.

"Blueberry is definitely calling my name." She takes a bite of one while walking over to where I am, leaning her back against the counter next to me. Taking a sip of my coffee, the Makana community calendar on the wall that nobody has bothered to wipe clean yet catches my eye.

"That's kind of a sad reminder, isn't it?" I cross the room and grab the eraser to start clearing the open house and showing appointments on the board.

"It is," she agrees sadly through bites of her muffin. As I wipe the rest of it down, my mind starts wandering and brainstorming different ways for me to advance at work in the new year—or to at least make it more of a challenge. There's usually a bit of a surge in listings once the holidays die down, so the potential uptick in workload is promising. There's also always the possibility of branching out into the corporate side of real estate or even delving into the developing side, so there are definitely other ventures to explore if I want to. I just need to decide which route would be best for me.

"A penny for your thoughts," Tori says quietly from behind me. I place the eraser on the ledge and turn to offer her a smile, crossing the room.

"Just thinking about my next moves," I reply. "Career-wise."

"Have you thought about opening your own firm?" she asks in a hushed voice, keenly aware of where we are.

"I have," I say with a nod. "That's definitely appealing to me. It's one of my long-term goals anyway. I just need to lay out all the risks and benefits of all my options and zero in on what makes the most sense, I guess."

"I can help you do that if you want? I'm a great brainstormer."

"You are." I pull her in for a side hug, giving her upper arm a squeeze. "And I would love that, thank you."

"You're welcome. It'll have to be later, though. I'm heading out for a meeting in about five minutes."

"Sounds good. I'm heading over to see my grandparents right now anyway," I say, reluctantly releasing her.

"Oh, tell them hi from me, please?"

"Will do." I grab my coffee mug from the counter as she grabs another muffin, and then I follow her back out of the break room.

"Sit, honey," Grandma says, pointing to an empty chair at their kitchen table. I slide into a seat as she shuffles to the countertop, picking up a red-and-green plastic tray and bringing it back, setting it in front of me.

"Did you do your baking today?" I ask. Every year, she devotes one full day to baking a wide assortment of holiday cookies that she shares with her friends and family in the last few days leading up to Christmas. I can always count on some fresh homemade cookies this week when I drop off their produce.

"I sure did. Can't you tell by the layer of flour on every surface of my kitchen? Mabel came over to bake, too, when she ran out of sugar. Who runs out of sugar this time of year?" she ponders as she slides into a chair of her own, right across from Grandpa.

I take a closer look at the kitchen, now noticing the mixing bowls, utensils, and random ingredients spread out across the counter. It looks like a tornado ripped through this place.

"Mabel didn't steal the snowball cookies, did she?" I ask, inspecting the tray that has a mixed variety of shortbread cookies, snowballs, and white chocolate macadamia nut cookies.

"She got her own tray. Don't worry," she replies.

"Ah, thank you. You do know the way to my heart," I say.

"You'll have to share your snowball recipe with Tori," Grandpa says to Grandma.

"Oh, yes," she replies, lighting up.

I don't miss how the mention of Tori's name makes me feel lighter almost instantly. Not that I was feeling heavy or down at all beforehand, but that's just what happens when I think about her. She has somehow infiltrated every nook and cranny of my life, never far from my mind, and it's kind of ridiculous how happy that's been making me.

"Speaking of Tori, I suppose you should know that we're officially dating," I say, figuring now is a good time to fill them in.

"Oh, we know," Grandma says with a questioning look. "We've met her several times now, remember?"

"Well, I know, but we weren't dating when I first brought her over here," I explain, wondering if it's even worth it to try.

"Sure, honey." She waves her hand, dismissing me as she heads back into the kitchen.

"She's a keeper, that one," Grandpa says with a nostalgic tone. "Ah, to be young and in love."

"Got any advice for me?" I ask. For once, I don't feel rushed or in a hurry to leave. I'm actually eager to soak up some wisdom on relationships from him. I'll take any tips I can get to not screw this up with Tori.

He leans back in his chair, and his shoulders lift with a deep inhale, looking introspective as he tilts his head. "Oh, let's see. I know everyone says it, but communication is key. Always put family first. And tell her you love her. A lot. Like this... Betty," he shouts her name, his voice shaking ever so slightly. He smiles broadly when she looks over at him from the sink.

"I love ya." He says it with such intention and emotion as if he hasn't said the same three words for the last sixty-five years.

"Love you too, Louie," she says just as softly before rambling on about the latest cafeteria gossip. He watches her go on with a blank expression.

"And just let her talk," he whispers, leaning over the table. "Eventually, you won't be able to hear her anyway."

With a laugh, I nod my head. "Thanks, Gramps."

"Oh, and find something you both love to do so you can do it together, but also do things by yourself still, too."

"I like that one," I say, nodding as I bite into a cookie.

"Do you love her?" he asks, searching my face for an answer.

I take a deep breath in and blow it out slowly. I've never been in love before—never allowed myself to get that far in a relationship—but the way I feel about Tori is nearing the point of overwhelming. Even when I'm focusing on work, she's still always in the corner of my mind, constantly providing comfort and a steady stream of happiness just from the simple fact that she exists. And when I'm with her, I'm consumed by her, just happy to be in her orbit.

"I think so," I admit to him, feeling a heat rush over my cheeks at the admission. He studies me with a smile.

"Judging by the look on your face when you were thinking about it, I would have to agree. You don't need to rush too fast or even tell her right away, but promise me that you'll keep her, okay? You should hang onto anything that makes you feel like that."

"Feel like what?" Grandma asks, coming back to the table. Grandpa shakes his head, and I appreciate when he doesn't involve her in the conversation—that it was a special thing meant just for us.

"Nothing, dear," he tells her.

"Are we all ready for Christmas?" Grandma turns her attention to me. "I promise to have this place cleaned up by then." My parents and I always come over here on Christmas Day so these two don't have to travel anywhere. We bring all the food so she doesn't have to cook, but my grandma prides herself on having a spotless home for us to celebrate in.

"I'll come by tomorrow afternoon and help you clean," I offer.

"That would be wonderful, sweetheart. Thank you. Will Tori be joining us on Christmas Day?"

"I'm not sure yet. I know she has her own traditions with her family, so we'll see how it plays out. We haven't talked about it yet."

"Are you going to ask her today? Then she can make plans," she points out.

"We'll see, Grandma," I reply.

"I know she mentioned liking to bake. Does she bake anything special for Christmas?"

"I don't think she's done any baking yet," I say, starting to feel a bit tired from all of the questioning.

"What did you get for her gift?" she asks eagerly, and I'm suddenly questioning if it was a smart move to stay here so long. "Louie got me a beautiful broach on our first Christmas together. Still have that thing too."

"That's nice. I don't know yet, but I'm sure I'll think of something," I brush it off.

"Betty, let the boy breathe," Grandpa interjects.

"I'm sorry, dear," she says to me with a smile. "I'm just in the holiday spirit, I guess."

"No problem, you know I don't mind. But I do need to head out," I say, planting a kiss on both of their heads and grabbing my cookie tray. "I have to get back to the office for a few things."

"Alright, thanks for the lovely visit, Connor, dear," Grandma says while walking me to the door.

"You don't need to walk with me every time I leave, Grandma. I know where the door is," I say with a laugh.

"It's just manners, dear. I've been seeing my guests out for sixty-odd years now. I ain't stopping now."

I wave one last time before closing the door behind me, shaking my head in both amusement and adoration. When the elevator takes me back down to the first floor, instead of rushing past, I stop to say hi to Ruth and give her a cookie before heading out the doors.

34

———————

TORI

"Do you think we're in trouble?" I ask Connor as we walk past the rows of cubicles toward Brad's office. "Does he know about us? There's no rule against inter-office dating, but maybe he frowns upon it. I can't remember now. Does he frown upon it?"

"Hey." Connor grabs the side of my arm and pulls me to a stop. He searches my face as he gently squeezes my arm, clearly picking up on my spiraling nerves. "It'll be fine. Whatever he wants to talk to us about, we'll figure it out, okay? Together."

I nod, trying to quiet the million questions that have been running through my head ever since Brad sent an email to us this morning saying he wanted to see both of us as soon as possible. Did we do something wrong? Am I going to wind up needing to choose between my job and this new relationship with Connor? I take a deep breath, focusing on him and letting the calmness behind the dark-green rim of Connor's eyes relax me and quiet my mind.

"Okay," I whisper before following him the rest of the way to Brad's office, where he knocks on the door and throws me one last reassuring smile when we're called in.

"Connor. Tori. Come on in and have a seat." Brad gestures to the two chairs that sit at the head of his desk. I can't get a good read from his tone as to whether this will be a positive or negative talk. Connor lets me pass, and I lower myself into the chair on the right.

"I suppose you're wondering why I called you in here today, huh?" Brad smiles warmly, which instantly helps to quell some of the lingering anxiety but only further amplifies the confusion.

"Do we get consolation trophies for the Makana competition?" Connor jokes, and I wonder how he can be so easy-going all the time—and especially at a time like this.

"Not quite," Brad chuckles, twisting the tip of a pen between his fingers, looking back and forth between the two of us. "But it does have to do with the competition."

My eyebrows lift up cautiously as I'm feeling surprised and confused at the same time, not quite understanding what he could possibly need to tell us.

"Okay," I reply, intrigued, lacing my fingers together and laying my clasped hands on my lap, trying to contain the nervous energy.

"I don't feel the need to reveal too many details, and what I do share, I would appreciate if we could keep between us. But long story short, Rich is no longer the winner of the competition," he says calmly.

"What?" Connor asks, slightly leaning forward in his chair, looking just as confused as I am.

Brad clears his throat and leans back, crossing his arms over his chest. "I was made aware that Rich offered your potential clients a home buyer rebate. He offered them five percent of the sales price in cash after closing if they worked with him."

"Seriously?" I ask, shock and anger swirling in my gut. I

knew something fishy had to have happened, but hearing the details makes me nauseated.

"Unfortunately, yes. Now, obviously, this isn't illegal, and it's commonplace for many agents to do it. It isn't so much the simple fact that he offered it, but I personally don't like how he did it to steal your buyers away from you and to entice them to sign with him." He shifts forward. "Long story short, I've been able to smooth things over with the buyers, and they're still eager to purchase Makana Manor. I'm not thrilled with how they went about this either, but at the end of the day, I just want this listing wrapped up and out of my hands."

My mind feels hazy as I process everything that he's saying. Rich is officially out, but Sarah and Micah are still buying the house?

"That being said, I'm now declaring you two as the rightful winners of the competition." He points to both of us.

My jaw drops open, and my eyes go wide, shock and excitement suddenly overpowering any anger I was just feeling.

"Really?" Connor asks excitedly.

"Yup, and honestly, rightfully so. You put all the work in and formed a relationship with these clients in the first place, so it belongs to you. Congratulations. You'll receive the commission on this listing and the additional bonus." He smiles broadly, clearly happy for us.

I fight the urge to jump in Connor's lap and give him a hug, but common sense wins out, and instead, I settle for a grin.

"Oh my gosh." I cover my mouth with my hands, a stray giggle escaping.

"Thank you." Connor stands to shake Brad's hand, and I follow, doing the same.

"You earned it." Brad smiles at us. "Now, I do expect you to keep things professional with Rich, please. I don't want any more drama in the office. I'll deal with him and his behavior, okay?"

"You got it." I nod, already determined to not let the mention of Rich ruin my celebratory joy.

"I don't mean to kick you out, but I do have another meeting in ten minutes. We'll be in touch soon, okay?" Brad says.

"Thank you," I say again as we make our way to the door. I'm just about to shut it behind me when his voice causes me to pause in my tracks.

"Oh, by the way, I know all about the two of you," Brad says as he's already sifting through paperwork, head down and the smile completely gone from his face. My stomach drops briefly, wondering how this will play out.

"Keep it professional at work, and we won't have any issues," he says simply and firmly.

"You got it," Connor says right before I pull the door shut.

We walk briskly back to our cubicles, unable to hide our grins, and I fight the urge to grab his arm the whole time. When we make it to our desks, I slide into my chair. Connor pushes his chair back slightly and reaches a hand out to me. We've been keeping any PDA at a minimum while we're at the office, but I cave and reach my hand out to squeeze his. When we let go, he reaches for his phone and types away briefly. My phone vibrates with an incoming text message almost immediately.

Connor: I don't want to say anything out loud because I don't want word to spread quite yet, but congratulations, Tori.

I smile, biting the side of my lip, looking back over at him briefly before typing back.

Tori: Congratulations to you as well, Connor.

Connor: We need to celebrate. Tomorrow?

> Tori: Tomorrow is Christmas Eve. Don't you have plans?

> Connor: Nope. My parents won't come over until Christmas Day, so tomorrow is usually free for me. What about you? It's okay if you have other plans. We can do it another time.

> Tori: I actually don't have any plans either. My family members all go to their significant other's families, so I was just going to hang out with Matt and Paige.

> Tori: But I'd rather be with you.

> Connor: Then it's a date. A Christmas Eve date.

> Tori: Sounds perfect. I don't even care what we do as long as champagne is involved. We just won a very important competition, Connor Brooks, and I must have champagne.

> Connor: Hell yeah, we did. There will most definitely be champagne. Now quit smiling at me and get back to work before we get in trouble.

With a laugh, I close out my phone and steal one more glance his way before touching the mouse pad to wake up my computer. The rest of the day is spent finishing up any last-minute odds and ends in anticipation of taking the next two days off, and I can't for the life of me wipe the silly grin off my face the entire time.

35

———————

CONNOR

"This was the perfect day," Tori says from beside me in my backyard pool, where we're leaning our elbows on top of the ledge, champagne flutes in hand. The pool lights cast a light-blue glow over our bodies that are submerged in the water from the chest down. The air is starting to have a slight chill to it now that the sun is almost all the way down.

"It really was," I agree, clinking our glasses together in a toast. My fingers are pruney from being in the pool for so long, so the stem of the glass feels a little bit awkward against my skin. I had suggested several festive date ideas and outings for us to do today, but the more we talked about our options, the more we knew that anywhere we went would be crawling with people, and we both gravitated toward being alone today.

After spending the night together last night, we spent the morning at her place, where I helped her organize all her Christmas cards into shoe boxes. For whatever reason, she hates the idea of throwing any of them away, so she's storing them all, which I don't pretend to understand, but I think it's sweet. We ended up heading back to my place, where we grilled a late lunch of chicken and veggies and have since spent the entire rest of the day in my pool—aside from when we briefly got out to order the sushi that now sits next to our champagne.

"Do you think there's a record for how long someone has stayed in a pool?" she asks, popping a sushi roll in her mouth.

"Probably," I reply. "Should we try and beat it?"

"Yes," she says definitively, finishing her bite and pushing away from the ledge, floating through the water. I follow slowly after her instinctively—something that I do without even thinking. We've been following each other around like a cat and a mouse in this pool for hours now, neither one of us wanting to be very far apart. She glances back, watching me as I sink lower, preparing to go under the water.

"Oh no, not again!" she squeals with a knowing expression, attempting to hurry away. I dip all the way under the water, pulling my eyes slightly open, just long enough to find her body frantically swimming away in the other direction. I swim deeper, finding and gripping her thighs. I use my feet to push the both of us upward off the floor of the pool. I push my arms above my head once we're out of the water, launching her high into the air. I laugh as she yells, kicking her feet mid-air, and flops into the deep end of the pool with a big splash.

"Why do you have to keep doing that?" She laughs breathily when she surfaces, smoothing the hair out of her face.

"I like when you get mad," I tease, not moving an inch even though she's advancing on me with a forced display of anger on her face.

"You're lucky I kind of like you, or I would not be putting up with this treatment." She uses her hands to splash a wall of water in my face, which I shake from my face with a laugh.

"Come here," I say, reaching my arm out to slide it around

her waist, pulling her closer to me. She willingly comes all the way in, wrapping her legs around my waist. I hold her steady, hands on the backs of her thighs, while she lets her arms hang off to her sides, hovering on top of the pool water.

She tilts her head up to the sky, and I'm immediately zoned in on the way she looks. On the outline of her sun-kissed face and the dampness of the pool water sliding across her skin. I'm completely entranced by her inhibition and how she looks when she's this carefree. My chest squeezes, filled with emotion, and all of a sudden, I'm swallowing back the impulse to tell her that I love her. It's crucial that she knows that.

But on second thought, I'm self-aware enough to know that I'm definitely feeling the effects of the champagne, and I know for a fact that she is too, judging by the flush on her cheeks. She deserves an intimate, intentional moment between just the two of us, not a spontaneous half-tipsy one, so I bite my words back.

"What time do you need to get back?" I ask, watching as she brings her head back to meet me straight on. "Do you need to be at your parents' pretty early tomorrow?"

Her eyes pierce mine, and she brings her hands around my neck before shaking her head. "We don't gather until around nine or so in the morning. You? You're usually on your own, right?"

"Yeah." I hold her gaze before nodding and saying softly, "But I'd rather not be."

"Same," she whispers, her eyes lazily searching mine. The air between us feels thick and charged with lingering electricity that has me drawing closer to her.

"Stay with me tonight?" I ask as I move in even closer, lifting my eyes to hers.

She smiles and nods, not even bothering to verbalize an answer. I press my mouth to hers with a firm yet gentle pressure, and we share a deep, slow kiss. When we part, she visibly shivers. I'm not sure if it's the effects of the kiss or from the chill in the air, but either way, I tilt my head in the direction of the house.

"We should probably go in, huh?" I ask.

She nods reluctantly. "I suppose." We untangle from each other and start swimming for the stairs.

"We definitely would not have won the world record for staying in a pool. That was kind of pathetic," I laugh, reaching for the towels that hang over the arm of a chair.

"Well, we tried." She shrugs. "But my pruning skin takes priority over some record."

We grab our champagne and empty sushi containers and walk through the sliding doors into my house. There's now a cozy rug right inside the door, so we wipe our feet before continuing on into the kitchen. After setting everything on the counter, I lead Tori down the hall to my bedroom.

"Do you mind if I borrow something to wear?" she asks, walking toward my closet.

"Take anything you want," I reply, pulling a dry pair of shorts out of my drawer for myself. I offer her a pair of gray sweatpants, which she happily accepts. She pulls out a long-sleeve black thermal shirt from my closet and shuffles to the bathroom to change.

I'm back in the kitchen, wearing sweatpants and a T-shirt, making popcorn, when she emerges from the hallway, my oversized clothes somehow looking extremely sexy as they hang off her small frame. Her hair is damp and curly as it hangs loosely off to one side. I don't look away, and she walks in my direction as if her body is responding to the force of my mind that's willing her closer.

"Hi," she says, cheerfully planting a kiss on my cheek and squeezing my forearm as she walks by, pulling the champagne out of the fridge.

"You know this is kind of serious, right? Spending Christmas

Eve together?" she asks as she refills our glasses, and I shake the contents of the popcorn bag into a large bowl.

"Yeah. Well, I'm low on options, and you're better than being alone," I tease, walking behind her to the couch in the living room. She throws me an exaggerated eye roll before settling down onto the couch.

I take the open spot next to her, handing the popcorn over so I can grab the blanket that's hanging over the back to drape over us.

"Oh, wait." Tori jumps off the couch and plugs the Christmas tree in, turning the overhead light off before coming back and laying her legs over my lap under the blanket. She places the popcorn bowl in the middle so we can both reach it.

"You can pick the movie," I tell her, using the remote to scan through the various options.

"Ooh." She taps my arm when *Elf* comes up as an option. "I love this one."

"You got it." I press play, setting the remote down, and we stay snuggled up on the couch under the blanket, sipping champagne and eating popcorn while watching the movie. All the while, I feel content and happy. I can't help but think back to Christmas Eve last year when I was all by myself, catching up on work, with absolutely no idea what I was missing out on.

36

TORI

"Merry Christmas, Tori," Elliot says, planting a kiss on my cheek. He steps on a crumpled ball of discarded wrapping paper, creating a loud crunching noise as he makes his rounds around the living room.

"Merry Christmas, Elliot," I say, but I'm not entirely convinced that he heard me as he's already moved on to say thank you to Ava. My parents' living room is completely trashed, a jumbled mix of people, presents, and discarded bows and tissue paper. The girls are camped right in the middle of the chaos, tearing open freshly unwrapped gifts. Emily is admiring her gift —a hanger with the word *bride* that her wedding dress will hang on. It was a gift from Grace, who's attempting to shove some trash into a large garbage bag.

Christmas morning is one of my absolute favorite days of the whole year. The one day that the outside world stops, and I get to enjoy the people that I love, watching them light up over and over with each gift opened.

"One more present for you, Elliot," Matt says, emerging from the hallway with a large wrapped box in his hands. Elliot's face lights up as soon as he sees it.

"What is it?" he asks, jumping up and down.

"Open it," Matt says with a grin, laying the box gently in the middle of the floor.

We all watch as Elliot opens the top of the box slowly before throwing it off altogether, revealing a small black lab puppy.

"A puppy!" he shouts. The excitement on his face and in his voice is contagious, and we all cheer and shout with joy for him. Matt lifts the puppy out of the box, setting her in Elliot's lap once he sits on the floor.

"Her name is Moxie, but you can choose a different name if you'd like," Paige says from the couch, a huge smile on her face, her eyes getting misty.

"Moxie's perfect," he says dreamily, petting her in his lap. A lone tear runs down his cheek as he looks at both Paige and Matt. "Thank you. I'll take good care of her, I promise."

"We know you will, buddy," Matt says, ruffling his hair.

My eyes tear up, watching the emotion in Elliot's face, and I excuse myself to the kitchen to grab a tissue. While I'm dabbing at my eye, I glance at my watch and realize that I should be leaving soon if I want to make it to Connor's grandparents' place.

"Are you heading out?" Mom asks, strolling into the kitchen.

"Yeah, I should probably get going. Thank you for such a great morning." I hug her neck and give her a kiss on the cheek.

"You're welcome, Tori. Say hi to Connor for us," she says with a knowing smile.

"I will."

"Hey, Tori," Mom stops me before I make it out of the

kitchen. When I glance back at her, she smiles. "You look happy."

I return the smile with one that I feel all the way down to my soul. "I am. Merry Christmas, Mom."

Back in the living room, I say goodbye to the rest of my family members individually, giving each of them a hug. I load up and carry my basket of newly opened gifts out to my car.

I make my way along the coastline on the nearly empty road, the beach and the sidewalks void of people, the food trucks and beachside bars all closed. When I arrive, I grab the presents I need out of my trunk, along with the tray of raspberry-cheesecake bars I made, and make my way in and up the elevator. Connor comes out into the hallway before I even make it to their door. A blast of loud Christmas music pours out of their unit behind him before he pulls the door shut.

"Hi," he says with a smile, kissing me on the cheek. "I wanted to give you this in private before we go in. It's loud in there."

"Okay," I laugh. He lowers himself onto the floor with his back against the wall. I set my gifts on the floor before sliding down to sit next to him, extending my legs out in front of me.

"I got you something too," I tell him, starting to reach for his gift before he stops me.

"Mine first." He hands me a small red gift bag. I smile, pulling out some tissue paper to reveal a smaller circular object that's neatly wrapped in tissue paper.

"Wow, nice job wrapping," I say, pulling it out.

"To be fair, my grandma wrapped it," he says nonchalantly.

"You made your elderly grandmother wrap it for you?" I elbow him in the ribs.

"Tori, you've met her. She insisted," he says, looking at me as if that should have been obvious.

Shaking my head in amusement, I use my finger to pull at the tape, pulling it open to reveal a beautiful gold bracelet.

"Oh Connor, I love it," I breathe, moving it around in my hand, watching it glimmer even with the harsh fluorescent lighting of the hallway. "It's so beautiful."

"Look at the charm," he says. I lift the bracelet higher, grabbing the small charm that hangs slightly off of it and flipping it over to reveal an imprint of a stamp.

"A stamp?" I ask, confused. His proud grin grows wider.

"To remind you of all your Christmas cards that you got this year and the nice gesture that Elliot made."

My heart bursts with emotion, and I bring a hand to rest against my chest.

"And to remind you that you're never alone," he says softly.

With that, I set the bracelet down and turn to Connor. I gently grab his chin with the tips of my fingers and give him a kiss before looking intently into his eyes.

"Thank you. I absolutely love it," I say sincerely.

"You're welcome," he says, giving me one more kiss.

"Okay, your turn." I let go of him, slide the bracelet on my wrist, then hand him a white-and-silver square box. He smiles as he quickly rips it open, revealing an assortment of ornaments nestled in straw paper.

"To start off your ornament collection," I tell him, watching as he pulls each one out. There's a house ornament with the words *Makana Manor* handwritten on the bottom. A baseball bat ornament is tucked in the corner, right next to a glass paddleboard. And a hot chocolate mug ornament is hidden beneath a Santa hat. Several more are nestled underneath, each with some sort of relevance to the last month that we've spent together.

"Tori," he breathes. "I love them. So much."

I smile happily as he sets the box down on his lap and comes in for another kiss.

"Thank you," he says against my lips, using his free hand to grip my leg just above my knee.

"You're welcome," I whisper back when he rests his

forehead against mine. "We should probably head inside before they start wondering where you are, huh?"

"Yeah, I suppose," he agrees with a sigh. He stands and helps me up before we grab our gifts and head inside.

"Tori! Merry Christmas," Betty says when she sees me, arms widening for a hug.

"Mele Kalikimaka," Lou chimes in from his spot on the couch, and I make my way around the room, greeting both of them and Connor's parents.

"I brought some treats, although I'm sure they're nowhere near as good as yours," I tell Betty as I set the tray on the kitchen counter.

"Oh, they look delicious!" Connor's mom says before offering me a mug. "Would you like some coffee?"

"Sure!" I take the mug, pour myself a cup, and follow both of them back to the living room to get settled between Connor and his grandpa on the couch, watching as they hand out more gifts and banter back and forth about which gift belongs to who.

And I spend the rest of Christmas Day celebrating with his family, complete with loud music, loud conversations, and being glued to the side of the best gift I could have ever asked for.

37

TORI

"Look out. Jellyfish." Connor points to a spot in the ocean by our feet, his voice monotone and lacking any sense of urgency.

"What?" I squeal, jumping to lift my feet out of the ankle-deep water. "Where?"

"I'm kidding," he laughs apologetically.

"Not. Funny." I slap him on his chest while he tries to dodge my attack.

"I'm sorry," he says again. "That was not funny—in no way, shape, or form whatsoever."

"I was stung by a jellyfish when I was seven, and it scarred me for life," I explain, still breathing heavily.

"I'm sorry," he says yet again, squeezing my hand to pull me closer to his side. He lets go of my hand and throws his arm over the top of my shoulders, pulling me the rest of the way until I'm pressed right against him. I reluctantly throw my arm around his waist, sliding a finger through his belt loop, knowing that I can't stay mad at him for long. My blue sundress ruffles with the wind, brushing against Connor's gray shorts as we walk.

We packed a picnic earlier for our beach date this evening, and after a long day of work, we walked from the office to the beach—towels, beach bag, and picnic basket in tow. The only thing we forgot were swimsuits, so here we are, still in our work clothes, feeling slightly overdressed as the sun bares its heat on us.

"Ah!" I jump at a small clump of sand that moves in the water by my ankle. "You've got me all paranoid now."

"Here," he says, crouching down low, signaling for me to hop on his back. "I'll save you from the non-existent jellyfish."

"I have a dress on," I point out. He stands, studying me for a moment, and then places one arm behind my shoulder blades, and the other he wraps around the backs of my knees, swiftly lifting me until he's carrying me sideways.

I squeal, throwing my arms around his neck as he easily carries me through the ankle-deep water, eventually veering out and onto the sand. My fingers slide between the collar of his lightweight button-up shirt as I try to keep my grip. He leads me toward our spot on the beach, where my picnic basket is sitting on his red beach towel.

"Okay, put me down. You're starting to get sweaty," I laugh before he lowers me onto the sand, and I walk the rest of the way. Once at the towel, I sit down and pull the mini cooler that has our sandwiches and lemonade out of the basket.

"Did I tell you that Matt invited us over to his bar for a New Year's Eve celebration tomorrow?" I ask, passing a turkey sandwich to him. "The whole group will be there, I guess. Quinn will be home, so it would be fun to see her."

"That sounds like fun," he says, taking a bite. "Way more fun than the bridge tournament going on at the assisted living facility."

"Oh, I forgot about that. We definitely need to make an

appearance there."

"Tori, we do not need to spend our New Year's Eve celebration with my grandparents," he says with a pointed smile, leaning back on one elbow so he's sprawled out on his side, half-eaten turkey sandwich in one hand.

"Yes, we do. We'll play bridge for a couple of hours before heading to Matt's. How does that sound?" I say confidently.

"Works for me," he says in a way that tells me he's happy to just be along for the ride. His phone rings in his pocket, and I watch as he sets his sandwich down, brushes the crumbs off his fingers, and reaches for it. He pauses to glance at me, and he answers the phone when I give him a reassuring nod.

"This is Connor," he says, switching to his professional tone of voice. I think back to when Rich called us on the way to the beach earlier to officially apologize for his actions regarding Makana. As much as I'm still irritated and wary when it comes to him, I do appreciate the gesture and am mature enough to move on.

I eat the rest of my sandwich, watching the waves crash to shore while he finishes his phone call. He hangs up after no more than five minutes, shifting his attention back to me. I love that we've gotten to a point where work is still a priority for both of us, but there's a strong sense of balance. We're both able to prioritize and make time for important things in our lives—both professionally and personally—and I'm proud of us for getting to this place.

"That was Scott. Remember I told you about him?" he asks. "He does commercial real estate on the island? Anyway, he says he found a small office building that the owner will be looking to lease in about six months. He said it's exactly what I'm looking for."

"Oh, that's great! When will you go see it?"

"Probably tomorrow. If I like it, I'd love to sign an agreement to lock it down while I get my licensing exams done and everything else in order these next few months. Want to come with me to see it?"

"I'd love to," I say with a smile. Connor made the decision to go through the additional steps of getting his broker license and opening up his own firm. I'm proud of him for making this choice and pursuing this dream to further his career. It's definitely a step in the right direction to figuring out what more he wants from his professional life. I'm just happy to be along for the ride and support him in any way that I can.

We finish eating in silence and clean up our towel before Connor moves to position himself in the middle of it, patting the space in between his knees.

"Come here," he says softly and intently at the same time. With a smile, I lower myself between his legs and scoot all the way back so that I'm lying against his chest, my head resting against the top of his left shoulder. I stretch my legs out in front of myself, and he raises his knees, resting his forearms against them by leaning forward slightly, effectively caging me in.

I sink into him and his body heat, not even caring that the air is already hot and muggy. We sit for a few quiet moments, just watching the roll of the ocean waves as they crash onto shore. A few surfers are in the water directly in front of us, and a catamaran boat is out in the distance, bobbing up and down with the waves.

I can feel Connor shift his head closer, tilting his chin into my hair. His breath gently hits the side of my neck before he whispers quietly.

"Tori?"

"Yeah?" I say, leaning my head back slightly so I can hear him better over the wind and the crashing of the waves.

"I love you," he says softly into my hair. It comes out in a tender, soothing kind of way that melts me to my core. My stomach swoops, and there's no stopping the grin that grows wild on my face. I twist my head the rest of the way so I can look him in the eyes, the back of my head resting on his upper arm.

"I love you too."

EPILOGUE

TORI

Eleven Months Later

"How about we take a break from packing?" I suggest, closing a box that's filled with home decor and sealing it shut with multiple layers of packing tape.

"Good idea," Connor agrees. He stands, abandoning a half-full box that sits in front of him on my living room floor. I follow him to the kitchen, where he grabs two wine glasses and a bottle of sauvignon blanc.

Before grabbing what I need, I take the most recent card we received in the mail that still sits on the counter and bring it over to the display wall. It's Matt and Paige's Christmas card with a picture of the four of them on the beach, Moxie sitting between Elliot and Noelle. Paige's pregnant belly is on full display. I use a clip to hang it right in between several other cards—one of Quinn and Brian on his fishing boat with a large mahi on the line. And another of John and Mia with their one-year-old boy, David, who they named after his late father. The last one I see is the card that my parents sent out, which is a large group picture of the whole family at Emily's wedding this past spring.

I love seeing cards displayed like this so I can see all of the people that mean the most in my life. I don't even care that I should already be packing them away—this will definitely be the last thing taken down before we go.

Grabbing a stack of our own cards to take with me, I follow him out onto the balcony. We assume our typical position with him leaned back on a chair and me in between his legs, my back against his chest. I scoot down so my head rests just under his chin, his knees bent next to my elbows.

"I can't believe we're officially moving in two weeks," I say excitedly before taking a sip of wine.

"Just in time for Christmas." He places a hand on my arm. "You sure you want to live with me? I could be a terrible roommate, for all you know. What if I leave socks everywhere and dirty dishes in the sink?"

"I know what I'm signing up for," I say confidently with a smile. We ended up pooling our competition prize money together to put a down payment on our first home together—a quaint beachside bungalow near Brian's Marina. Just a few houses down from Quinn. Although it'll be a chaotic couple of weeks getting moved in, we're both excited to spend Christmas in our first home together.

I set my glass on the table and grab the stack of cards, using my phone to pull up the master list of addresses, scrolling to where I left off.

"You sure you want to work on those right now? Why don't you take a break?" Connor says quietly from behind me.

"I don't mind. Plus, I'd really like to get these sent out soon," I say.

After getting the name of the Christmas card program from

Paige and Elliot, Connor and I decided to start our own tradition of sending Christmas cards to people around the world who might be lonely during the holiday season. I'm hoping it's one that we'll continue to do year after year.

I settle back against his strong torso, his arms curling around me as the last little slice of the sun disappears beneath the palm trees. The glow of the string lights along the railing give off a little bit of light, just enough to see the card as I address it.

Our card is a five-by-seven image with a collage of this past year together. One of us on paddle boards that Matt took at one of our family picnics. Another one of the two of us at Emily's wedding. One of us standing in front of the retail space that Connor leased. It's an image of the very first day that he officially started his own brokerage firm—with me being his first employee. And the last one is a selfie of us at Elliot's first youth baseball game.

This last year was filled with so many wonderful memories as we began our life together, and I can't help but smile when I look at our card and think of everything that's yet to come. With a sigh, I sign the bottom of the card.

With love from Oahu,
Connor and Tori

The End

ALSO BY MEGAN REINKING

The Hawaiian Getaway Series

The Ohana Cottage

The Summer Break

The Perfect Tide

The Holiday Prize

ACKNOWLEDGMENTS

First of all, a huge thank you to YOU, the reader, for reading The Holiday Prize! Whether this is your first time reading a book of mine, or if you have read all of my books, I deeply appreciate you taking a chance on me and supporting my dreams! My goal from the beginning of this book was to write a feel-good holiday romance that would spread some cheer and leave readers with that warm fuzzy feeling in their chest. I hope you enjoyed it as much as I enjoyed writing it!

A huge thank you to my husband, Nick, for your continued support and pushing me to follow my dreams. I love you! Thank you to my kids for giving me space when you know I need to write and for being so proud to tell your friends that your mom is an author. Love you big.

Thank you to all of my friends and family for your constant support and for cheering me on, in all the big and small ways that you do! It truly means the world to me!

Thank you to Jamie for being one of my biggest cheerleaders and one of the biggest reasons that I finish any book. Sharing my stories with you in their raw, unedited, messy first draft form always feels safe to me because I know that you will treat it with such kindness and gentleness. Your feedback and excitement means so much to me and always encourages me not to give up!

To my beta-readers—Lindsey, Erin, Shelby, Hannah, Jessee, Lexie and Brooke—I am beyond appreciative of your kind critique and feedback with The Holiday Prize! Each one of you brought a unique perspective, and I am so grateful for all of the ways you helped me fine-tune this story. You helped mold it into what it is today!

Thank you to my editor, Jenn Lockwood, for being so amazing! I am so appreciative of the work you put into editing this story!

To my cover designer, proofreader, and everyone else who had a hand in polishing this book—thank you!!

Lastly, to all of the readers, Bookstagrammers, BookTokers, and book bloggers, I cannot express how much your continued support means to me! Every single review, comment, share, etc. means the absolute world to me!

ABOUT THE AUTHOR

Megan Reinking is a wife and mother who lives in Minnesota, where she spends her days reading, writing, or chauffeuring her three children around town. She's a homebody who loves quiet, lazy days and connecting with family and friends.

.

www.ingramcontent.com/pod-product-compliance
Lightning Source LLC
Chambersburg PA
CBHW061249310726
48971CB00007B/2287